Praise for Author Carole Brown

Carole Brown is one of those refreshing authors who writes novels that keep you up at night. Whether you are reading one of her mysteries, historical suspense or romantic suspense novels, you won't be able to sleep until you find out what happens.

--Tamera Lynn Kraft,
Author of "A Christmas Promise" and
Resurrection of Hope"

Carole Brown has the literary ability to ferry you into the heart of each story, depicting each setting in exquisite detail, allowing you to follow along with the characters as they think, feel and discover. Though each novel is a masterpiece in its own right, Carole's distinguishable writing carries throughout everything she writes. One of the best up and coming suspense writers of our time.

--Jamin Baldwin,
Author and Freelance editor

Carole Brown writes with a touch of humor, just enough mystery-suspense to keep the reader turning the pages to see what happens next, and a nice mixture of sigh-worthy romance. Looking forward to the next book in the series.

Carol Ann Erhardt,
Christian Romantic Suspense author of
Joshua's Hope and the Havens Creek Series

Carole Brown does a wonderful job of balancing romance and mystery, keeping her readers engaged while at the same time entertained. This series is a good read for anyone who loves curling up with a good book, one that will cement your faith in happy endings.

--Barbara Derksen, author of the Wilton/Strait and Finder Keepers Mystery series

Cozy romance meets cozy mystery! Romance is in the air... Or is it? Mystery interwoven with a light-hearted romance makes this a book to snuggle with. Enjoy it with your fresh brewed cuppa coffee or not. Although romance is not my usual cuppa tea, I can certainly recommend this clean read with suspense that'll keep you guessing with every turn.

Emma Right, author of children and teen fantasy and mystery books.

Undiscovered Treasures

An Appleton, WV Romantic Mystery

Carole Brown

Story and Logic Media Group
Printed in the USA
... For the discriminating reader
...because we believe story *needs* logic.

Published by STORY AND LOGIC Media Group ... For the discriminating reader ... Because we believe story *needs* logic.

Cover Design by SAL media
Printed in the USA

ISBN 13: 978-1-941622-38-4
ISBN 10: 1941622380

Library of Congress Cataloging-in-Publication Data
Brown, Carole
Title: /Carole Brown
ISBN 978-1-941622-38-4 (pbk)

1. Series fiction 2. Cozy Mystery 3. Romance
4. Inspirational fiction

I. Title. Library of Congress Control Number: 2016955564

Dedication:

To Christina
for being one of my best fans
and for your enthusiasm and help
in promoting my books.

I love you!

Acknowledgments:

Thank you, God, for help
and strength to finish another book.
I couldn't do it without you.

To my fans who want more books:
Heavenly words!

To those who listen, and encourage,
and spend time critiquing, brainstorming,
and pushing me onward:
The simple words “thank you”
don't convey my appreciation.
You're the best!

Carole Brown

Undiscovered Treasures

An Appleton, WV Romantic Mystery

Chapter One

Andy whistled as he poured coffee in his favorite cup, grabbed a Greek yogurt and headed to his studio. It was early, but not too much so. Perfect lighting to work on his latest painting.

He nodded at his new assistant, but didn't speak, and shoved open the door to his work area. His gaze circled the room—as it always did.

His favorite place in the whole world. He sucked in a deep breath, inhaling the faint smells of the paints and turpentine, but he kept moving toward the window in the back of the room and stopped.

It was already open.

Had he shut it last night?

There was nothing disturbed that he could see, so...he shrugged. Time to get to work.

Andy took a sip of his coffee and flipped back the cover from his latest—and best—painting of Caroline Gibson.

The painting leered at him, as if it was a caricature transformed into monster life. Slashed into ribbons, with dashes of red, jarring paint splattered over it, his work was ruined. Beyond saving.

Belatedly, Andy set his cup down on a nearby table, and with a shaking hand, reached toward the damaged picture. He stepped back and wondered if this was the worst nightmare of his life.

True, he could paint another one, but she'd never see the passion he'd put into *this* one, see his heart in every stroke, and see the love he'd painted in every color.

Ruined.

Why would anyone do this? It wasn't valuable—except to him.

Worse, *who* hated him so much he'd wreck this kind of havoc on him?

Was there a grudge-bearing individual in the small town of Appleton who had hoped he would hurt him by doing this?

If so, then they'd succeeded.

Chapter Two

"I'm depressed." Caroline Gibson yelled as she staggered under the weight of the books she carried from the storage room.

Her brother didn't bother to look up from the computer where he typed. "You're always depressed."

"Am not. And if I could get some help around here, the storage room would get cleaned out faster."

Toby looked up then. "You're doing fine. I've got to go after those two other pictures Andy promised us."

Caro sniffed. "That's what's making me totally depressed. I cannot abide..." she loved the old-fashion word "...that man's drab paintings. Why doesn't he paint in pastels? Or something..."

The toe of her sandal caught the ragged edge of a floorboard, and she tripped. Caro tried to catch herself, floundered, held on to the books for a second, then let them go in a desperate effort to keep from hitting the floor. Again.

Ouch.

Lifting a hand to rub her arm where the edge of a counter had scraped it, she winced and opened one eye.

Silence, then Toby's head appeared at the end of the aisle. "Are you okay? Didn't break anything, did you?"

"I didn't break any bones, if that's what you're asking."

"I meant any of our treasures." He grinned when she scowled.

"It's all Andy's fault."

"How on earth do you figure that?" Toby huffed and rubbed his chin.

"If I hadn't been so depressed over those horrible paintings of his, I'd have seen the aggravating board."

Toby did laugh then as he walked away. "Yeah, yeah. You've tripped over the same board how many times?" He stopped at a shelf and twisted the key in the back of a ballerina music box. The tinny music began playing as the dancer twirled. Toby looked back at her. "There. Now you'll have something to listen to while you're lying there feeling sorry for yourself."

Caro started to sit up when a thin hand appeared in front of her eyes. Had she hit her head? Was she having a vision? She studied the hand. Tan. Stained fingers and well-kept nails. Altogether a rather nice one. She let her gaze lift to the owner of the hand.

"Need some help?"

Andy Carrington, artist of the paintings she'd just labeled horrible, bent over her, a concerned look on his lean face. His outstretched hand still dangled in front of her face.

Oops. She'd done it again. She gave him a sharp glance. He didn't look offended. His gentle features seemed as placid as they always did. Maybe she could squeeze out of any explanations for her vociferous declarations of hatred for certain paintings.

Ignoring his hand, she scrambled to her feet. He dropped to his knees just as she stood and began gathering the scattered books she'd dropped.

An exasperated puff of air escaped from between her lips. Should she get back down on the floor and help or walk off?

He always placed her in a dilemma. Why couldn't he peddle his work somewhere else? Just because Toby liked him didn't mean she had to, did it? Or that they had to display the stuff he called art in their shop.

Without a thought, she tapped a foot in agitation—or was it nervousness? Of course not!—and when Andy glanced at it, she cringed and walked away. Let the books stay on the floor.

She bent over Toby's shoulder as he pecked away at some chart on his computer and whispered. "Your friend's here. Probably with some of his ghastly art."

"Stop it, Sis." Toby's rebuke came with a severe look.

"Why?" Oh, dear. That perverse streak showed up every time she didn't want it to.

Toby sat back in his chair and sent her one of *those looks*. "Because you're not being nice. Because Andy's our friend. Because Andy is nice, and I don't want you hurting his feelings."

She tried for another sniff, then gave it up. After all, she really didn't want to hurt the man's feelings either. Hadn't Pastor Hagg just preached Sunday about being kind-hearted?

And she tried her level best, as her grandmother used to say when she was alive, to follow the Bible's teachings.

But it didn't mean she had to like his painting or want to deal with his puppy love. Why on earth couldn't he forget *her*?

Andy appeared around the aisle, his arms loaded with books. "Where do you want these, Caroline?"

"It's Caro, not Caroline." She waved vaguely at the old church bench that served as a catchall. "Put 'em there. Thanks."

"Hey, Tobe, how are things going?" Andy deposited the musty books.

Toby shut down the computer. "Good on my side. What're you doing in town on a weekday?"

"Needed a break. Brought those two paintings you wanted."

Caro shot Toby a dirty look.

Toby flashed a smug look back at her. *See how nice he is*, his eyes said.

Wimp, Caro flashed right back at him.

"You look kind of peaked. Are you sure you're feeling okay?" Toby stood.

"I'm fine. Just busy. Let me get those paintings."

"I'll help. Caro, how about rustling up some grub for us?" Toby baited her with his goofy imitational cowboy slang.

"What am I, your servant?" Caro frowned. Toby was the greatest amateur actor in town, but she hated it when he put on his wild west act.

The refrigerator didn't hold much. She'd neglected to restock it since her friend Starli's wedding. She hadn't had time to think about food.

Come to think of it, she was hungry. She looked at the contents with greater interest. Hmmm. Sandwiches would do. They had plenty of peanut butter in the cupboard. Pickles, bananas, and honey would serve as toppings. Nutritious and delicious.

She checked for mold, then sliced the last of the homemade bread, set the peanut butter jar on their small table. Perfect. Fit for a king. Not that the description fit either Toby or Andy.

She heard their pounding footsteps on the stairs and hurried to pour the ice tea.

After the blessing, Andy reached for two slices of the bread, smeared peanut butter lavishly, laced it with bananas, and took a big bite.

"Are you sure you're okay?" Toby bit into his own creation of a peanut butter sandwich.

"I've got a problem. I think."

Great. *He thinks.* Caro choked on the giggle and peanut butter combination preventing the snort of laughter threatening to erupt.

"What are friends for?" Toby grew expansive.

Toby was laying it on pretty thick, if you asked her. Almost as thick as the peanut butter glob he'd layered on his bread. Caro leaned back in her seat and slid a disgusted look in his direction.

Andy laid his sandwich down on his paper plate. "Someone's stealing my paintings."

"What?" Caro laughed, then bit her lip. Who on earth would want those ghastly things? But it was none of her business. Let Toby deal with it. Andy was his friend, after all.

"Yeah. I thought I'd misplaced the first one, but then when the second one disappeared, I knew someone was stealing them." A small frown wrinkled his forehead.

"Do you have any suspects?" Toby reached for the peanut butter.

"Not really. I mean, whom am I going to suspect?"

Andy shrugged, and Caro's glance stopped at the sight of his wide shoulders' movement. Andy kept talking, obviously unaware she'd given him the once-over.

"The mailman? The delivery guy? My assistant who's doing a great job of keeping me organized?"

"Well, someone's doing it, unless, of course, you're getting senile." Caro wanted to slap a hand over her mouth. Why couldn't she keep quiet? Andy would think she was really brilliant with that deduction.

Andy's gaze flashed to her, but he shook his head. "Since I'm still on this side of thirty, I doubt it. But you're right, someone is definitely doing it."

"You call the cops yet?" Toby poured a mound of honey on top of the peanut butter he'd spread on his second sandwich.

"Yes, I couldn't decide whether to or not for awhile. It's not as if my work is valuable. Yet."

Yet? Did he really think they would someday be so? Ha.

"What do you mean?" Errgh. Why was he so slow?

"There's only one thing I can think of. Chicago's Regency's has offered me a contract. A very good contract." His shy glance took in both brother and sister with his good news.

"Really? Great." Toby reached over and slapped his friend on the shoulder.

Great? No, more than that. Regency's was THE biggest retailer for talented work in Chicago. Supported by a store like them meant something big. Who knew where one could go from there? What influence their backing would mean for Andy?

But those paintings of his? What were they seeing that she missed?

Still, it never hurt to be polite. "Congratulations."

His eyes glowed a warm oak brown, and Caro felt herself smiling. Then she blinked. What was she doing? She felt almost friendly with the worst painter in West Virginia. Best to switch the topic back to the thefts. "So what are you thinking? Someone feels threatened and is trying to eliminate the competition? Or someone thinks they'll grab your work and make a mint when it gets valuable?"

"I haven't the foggiest. I am having a new security system put in. I guess there's not much else to do. Perrin Douglas convinced me, last week when I had dinner with them, to call the police and report it. They came by and looked things over, but they didn't sound promising."

"No. You can't leave it to the cops in this town." Caro stopped when Toby and Andy stared at her.

Her defenses rose when Toby's dark hazel eyes twinkled at her in mischief.

"Well, he shouldn't. I mean, how much can we trust the cops of this town after what just happened?"

"They're not all crooked, just because Roland was." Toby shook his head. "Look at Eddie. Good cop through and through."

"They wouldn't believe it though, till faced with the evidence. Even after all those threats Roland put Starli through." Caro shoved aside her plate, her hunger gone. What her friend had gone through with an abusive scoundrel like Roland with all his threats. Just like his brother had been, only Ryan had used physical force against Starli.

"Okay, say you're right. What can we do? I know nothing about investigating anything, and I don't think you do either." Toby layered his honey and peanut butter-slathered bread with pickles.

Caro held up a hand and ticked off her points. "First, we're above average in intelligence, wouldn't you say?"

Her brother burst into a guffaw. "Well, Andy and I are for sure. Not quite convinced a cute sister of mine is."

"Says you." Caro wrinkled her nose at him. "Who scored higher on their SATs at college?"

"Just because she got a college degree, she thinks she's got the right to brag." He gave her an exaggerated glare. "Go on."

With a smirk, Caro continued. "Secondly, I've read a lot of mysteries. And you guys aren't immune to that sort of thing. Why can't we figure it out any better than any other amateur? I say, let's try."

"Oh, brother." Toby used one finger to make a couple large circles by his head.

Thought she was crazy, did he?

"The next big Sherlock."

Andy laughed. "Maybe, but Caroline does have a point. Why shouldn't she try? I can't afford to keep losing paintings especially if Regency's predictions for my work comes true."

"It's Caro. That is exactly my third point. It has to be stopped, and if the cops aren't motivated to do something, then...?"

Toby looked from Caro to Andy, then back to his sister again. At last, he raised his hands, but a sly glint sparkled in his eyes. "Fine. Go to it. But I can't help. I'm making a quick trip to Charleston for an estate auction."

Caro eyed her brother. Was he up to something? Trying to throw Andy and her together? She wouldn't put it past him.

Yet the chance to solve a mystery intrigued her. She'd wanted to try her hand at it for a long time. Could she do it? She wouldn't know unless she tried. She threw a "I-know-what-you're-doing" glance at him. "Fine. I'll take care of things on this end."

The pleased expression rippling across Toby's face sent the hounds of doubt baying at her heels again, and she wanted to groan. Not again. Why couldn't her friends get it in their heads she and Andy would never be an item? Girlish, childhood crushes meant nothing in real, grownup life.

She weighed her options. Hanging around bad artist Andy—the guy who wanted more than friendship from her—against the chance of solving a mystery.

Yeah, she could handle it.

Chapter Three

Andy whistled as he hurried to his car and realized it was the same tune Caroline's ballerina music box played.

'*You're my everything...*' True enough, and she was.

Had he just snagged an accomplishment, or had he? How had he managed to secure days—even weeks—with Caroline? He wasn't as concerned about his pictures, although he hated to lose them, but Caroline definitely had been.

Thank you, God.

But hadn't God given him the verse he'd clung to for years?

And what we ask, we receive of him because we keep his commandments and do those things pleasing in his sight.

He'd lived his whole life trying his best to please God. He'd held onto the thought God would be pleased to give him the desire of his heart. That desire was Caroline Gibson.

How long had he adored her? He remembered her skinny legs wrapped around the horizontal tree branch, her pigtails dragging the ground as she swung upside down. Her little girl, angry voice had vibrated with determination. "*I can too do it as good as you.*"

A pang of regret stung him, and again he

sighed over how long he'd been trying to make up for those childhood days of teasing and taunting he and Toby had put her through. Turnabout was fair play, but it sure wasn't much fun.

Foolishness, trying to find who had stolen his pictures. They'd surely wind up somewhere. But so what? If it meant being with Caroline, well, he'd detect all night. If Caroline wanted it, so did he. Just so long as she never found out someone hated him—or was it her?--bad enough to destroy the painting of her.

He glanced over at the manila envelope lying on the seat beside him. The return address looked promising. More prospects for his future? More chances to make an impression on Caroline? To catch her attention?

He'd been patient long enough. Time to put feet to his prayers.

~*~

Back home, Andy tossed his mail on top of a large desk, flipped on lights, and went to pour himself a glass of orange juice. With a handful of veggies and a slice of carrot cake, he strode into his studio and sat down at his desk.

He needed to get started on another Caroline painting, *and* work toward finishing the next Regency painting due next month. But first...

He crunched on a carrot stick while he studied the intriguing manila envelope. The return address read the company he'd recently inquired about. If what their ad said was correct, he could make a pretty penny very quickly.

And money was what he needed. Along with prestige. He'd do anything to please Caroline. Anything.

Andy slid his letter opener beneath the envelope flap and pulled the letter from it. Papers and photos spilled out. He lifted the top sheet and read the letter.

"Dear Mr. Carrington,

We have reviewed your application and are interested in talking with you.

We would appreciate you looking over the material we have enclosed so you might get an idea of what type of art we're seeking.

We have viewed some of your work here in Chicago. You have amazing talent, although, of course, what we want needs to be much more exotic. Please understand our artists are in high demand, and we are prepared to offer what we are sure is higher than most artists can command.

Once you have reviewed the papers, please email your resume to us. Again, as we have already checked out your work, the process should be considerably reduced.

We are looking forward to hearing from you. Please contact us at ..."

Andy dropped the paper as excitement surged through him. This was his chance. His big chance, he was sure. This, along with the Regency opportunity—which would be a slower process—would surely get his name out there. And out there meant money.

Not that money meant much to him. It was great to have and use, but he'd be perfectly satisfied just to paint—and have Caroline by his side.

But if getting her meant having money and fame, then he'd do his best to give her what she wanted him to have and be.

Now, to his resume. He'd have Stephanie—his new and capable assistant—type an up-to-date one. What else? Maybe he should advertise for some girls to sit as subjects. He could send in some samples of his work. They wanted something "exotic," they'd said? He'd give them exotic. A few ads in some of the bigger newspapers should produce some choices to go with.

He hesitated. Should he use the word *girls*? Or would women sound better? He bent his head and scratched out a few lines, then sat back and read what he'd written.

Females needed to sit for an artist. Few hours a week. Please respond by calling: 555-3401.

That should do it. Stephanie—why did she seem familiar? Her avid denial was convincing, only the question continued to demand an answer in his brain. He'd wracked that organ, but couldn't ever remember a super blond. Ever. Other than Starli. One thing for sure, Stephanie's work since he'd hired her a month ago was excellent.

He must have caught the detecting bug from Caroline. That gave him a laugh. She would make an excellent detective. She had the confidence of almost everyone in town, and as a result, people confided in her.

Loyal and tender, she was a champion of the underdog. Probably got it from all those years of torment from Toby...and him. If he could only take it back. But he couldn't.

He refocused on his work. Time to write the ad himself and update his resume. Right now. Andy opened his computer and typed in the information. Hitting 'send,' he sat back.

The first step was done.

Chapter Four

Caro busied herself dusting the main selling area and waited on Andy to leave. Then she headed straight for Undiscovered Treasures' office.

She leaned on the door jam. "What do you think you're up to?"

Toby looked up, and if Caro didn't know better, she would have been sure surprise was the overwhelming expression on his face.

"What are you talking about?"

She didn't want to come out and say she suspected him of trying to throw Andy and her together. More ammunition for her mischievous brother to use. "You know. Why do you have to go to an auction right now? Why can't you stay and help find this thief? Aren't you even a little concerned? He's *your* friend."

His pencil dropped to his desk as he rubbed a hand across his face. "Sis, I go every year to this auction and find great buys. Plus the money we gain by selling off a few items here and there isn't anything to sneeze at. Just because you've suddenly got a bee in your bonnet about this theft thing, doesn't mean I have to get caught up in it. This is your problem now. You volunteered your expert detecting services. Now don't come whining to me for help."

That was really sweet out of an only brother. Caro sniffed. *Remind me never to depend on him for anything.*

"Personally, I think you—and Andy, too, for that matter—need to leave this to the cops. They may be blind when it comes to one of their own, but I'm sure they're going to do their best to find this thief."

"You don't have to be so snippy."

"I'm not trying to be. Just don't drag me into your escapades. I've got too much to do. Now leave me alone. I have work to do." Toby turned back to his computer.

Caro glared at him, then whipped around. She threw her next words over her shoulder at her brother. "Fine. I'll solve it by myself."

"Oh, yeah?"

Why did he always have to have the last word? Just because he was ten months older than her, didn't mean he knew everything.

Well, she could do this. What woman couldn't run a business, solve a mystery, write a few plays now and then, and keep a man in his place when he wanted more than friendship?

She settled herself on the barstool she used when she rang up their customer's purchases, pulled paper and pen from the drawer of the checkout desk and made a list.

First, she needed to check alibis: Andy's helper. What was her name? Stephanie Leason?

She remembered Andy laughing over suspecting the mailman, and true. They'd all known Jeffrey Sharp since they were kids, and she really didn't think Jeff would steal anything, but a real detective remained neutral. He, or she, as in this case, didn't rule out anyone unless he had the proof. She scribbled his name under Stephanie's.

She nibbled on the end of her pencil. Who else? What about Andy's neighbors? Let's see, on one side was the Norton couple and on the other was someone named Bennett. She knew the Nortons but had never met the Bennetts. Hmmm.

Who else? Caro scratched her ear. She couldn't think of anyone else to add to her list and frowned. Kind of skimpy for a list of suspects. She shrugged and moved on to her next item.

Check online for information about Regency's. She had no idea what for, but it sounded good.

Third, visit Andy's workshop to see if she could find anything incriminating—Caro loved the sound and repeated the word—incriminating there. If the cops had been there, she doubted if any clues had been left undisturbed, but who knew? Maybe she'd be smarter than the cops. Sounded exciting.

Maybe she should open a detective business. Advertise. She could choose what clients she wanted. Hey, she might even be so busy, she'd have to turn over Undiscovered Treasures to Toby to handle completely.

A pang at the thought stabbed her. Uh, no. She couldn't do that. She loved UT too much.

She sighed and studied her list. A half page. Not much to work with.

Well, she supposed she ought to study Andy's paintings a little. Try to see why someone would want to steal them. Ugh. What a chore. She had two right here that she could begin with.

Caro gave the pictures leaning against the wall a side-ways glance, then stood and strolled over to them. What was it that made the paintings so enticing to others that Andy's sales were soaring, and yet she wasn't any clearer on their meanings?

One was of a desert. Dry, barren, and desolate. Caro shivered. She slid her gaze to the next one. A storm brewing over some kind of water. Two people in a boat struggling to keep afloat. Ugh. She hated deserts, and she hated fierce storms.

Her head moved back and forth. She didn't get it. Was he a pessimist?

The bell over the door jingled, and Toni Deluca—she needed to remember Toni was now a Douglas—stepped inside. In her arms was her adopted baby girl, Dani.

"Hey, there, Caro." Toni dipped her head to plant a kiss on the top of dark-haired Dani's head. The baby gurgled and grabbed a fistful of Toni's hair.

"Hi. Isn't she a doll? Let me hold her." Caro stretched out her arms for the baby.

"Of course. Have you had lunch?" Toni looked around at the empty aisles. She picked up a small dish and examined it.

"I had to slave at getting lunch while Toby loafed in his office." Caro scowled, but when Dani puckered up, she made soothing noises and rocked back and forth.

"What did you have?"

"Well..." Caro hesitated and gave her friend

a sly look.

Toni crossed her arms and propped her chin on her fist in a thoughtful pose. “Let me guess. Cheese sandwiches and tomatoes.”

“Wrong,” Caro crowed. “Peanut butter with a choice of banana slices or pickles. Or if anyone wished to get creative, we had honey to flavor our peanut butter.”

“Caro. Caro.” Toni’s eyes warmed with love and laughter. “You can cook if you set your mind to it. You just don’t take the time to do it.”

“I really don’t like cooking much.”

“Did Toby enjoy his meal?”

“I’d say. He ate three sandwiches and Andy two.”

Toni lifted an eyebrow. “Andy ate lunch with you?”

“*I* didn't invite him. He dropped by with two more of his...ghastly paintings.” Caro nodded at the two pictures against the wall.

“I see.”

What did Toni see? “Toby invited him and ordered me to prepare lunch.”

“You know, there’s a deeper side to Andy most people don’t see. You know the old saying, ‘still waters run deep’?”

“We’ve known Andy all of our lives, Toni, and I haven’t seen anything remotely resembling mystery.” Caro looked down at the baby in her arms. A feeling of yearning spread through her. When would her handsome prince come riding up? When would her own children scream and laugh through her home?

“Oh, no, that's not what I mean. Andy’s not mysterious. I didn’t say that.”

"What on earth *are* you talking about then?"

Her friend's face was so peaceful, so content. *Mona Lisa in person.*

Slipping her arms around baby Dani, Toni gathered her up. "I have a feeling you'll soon be finding out a lot of things about Andy Carrington."

"What kind of things?"

"Did you hear there's a new girl in town?"

Was her friend evading her question? Hmmm. Sounded like it. "So?"

"So, I heard she's a beautiful extrovert who's won the heart of everyone she's met here in town." Toni placed another soft kiss on her baby's fuzzy hair. "And a red-head."

"And why should that mean anything to me?" Caro's skin prickled with irritation. She picked up her pad and studied her earlier scribbling on it.

Toni headed to the door. "Just that this red head's taken a liking to our friend Andy. She's throwing a small party at the hotel and invited Perrin and me. And Andy, of course."

"Don't go." Caro called after her. "You haven't heard about the thefts."

"Another time. I'm meeting Perrin for lunch."

The door of the shop slammed after her, then swung opened again, and Toni stuck her head back in. "I do want you do be as happy as I am with Perrin, and Starli and Joel are together. I'm praying that will happen soon."

"Ehhhh." Caro gritted between her teeth. Her arms felt empty, and the urge to solve a mystery did not include enigmas about herself.

What was Toni trying to say? That she should be happy with Andy Carrington? She didn't think so.

Who was this red head and why include Toni and Perrin and not her? Oh, well. She hoped he had lots of fun.

Toby strolled into the room carrying a suitcase. "I'm off."

"Now?" Caro wailed.

"Why not? Amy's going with me. She'll stay at her sister's, and I'll get a motel room. After the auction, we'll probably take a few days for fun."

"Why do you have to go now? You don't really have to buy anything. We've got tons of stuff ready to display when we have room." Why was she being so argumentative? She knew well enough when Toby made up his mind, there was no changing it.

"I want to go. I enjoy the buying." He set down his suitcase and pulled a stool closer to the counter. "Remember our bargain when we started this business together? I do the buying and book work. You run the business. Do you need to get away?"

Caro shook her head, and wisps of hair fanned around her face. "No, I don't want to go away. I just don't see why you can't help me with this thing of Andy's. He's your friend. I can't believe you don't care."

"I do care, and I love you for being concerned about my best friend. But I don't have the time or the desire to search for a thief. If you want to do that and have the time besides running UT, I'll cheer you on."

Caro had to concede he was right. Their agreement on running the shop had been a good one and worked well. Why was she complaining now?

She didn't think she'd better think that through. Time to agree and move on.

"You're right as usual. Sorry, Toby. I'm cranky. You're the best brother there ever was. Thanks for putting up with me."

Seriousness vanished, and the twinkle came back into Toby's eyes. "Oh, I figure it can't be for much longer. Someone's bound to come along I can bribe to take you away."

"Ooh, you." Caro swatted him with her notepad.

"Kidding." Toby held up both hands.

"You'd better be."

Toby pulled her close in a brotherly hug, patting her back. "God, you know our hearts. Please help us both to know and do your will. You know we love you."

Toby's whispered prayer in her ear was short and to the point, but tears stood in Caro's eyes when he'd finished. She hugged him. "Thank you, Tobe. You and Amy be careful and have a good time."

"And don't be putting yourself down so much. You're a little bit all right even if you are my sister." Toby headed for the door, then turned back. "You should give ol' Andy a chance."

Andy? Caro propped her arms on the counter. Why was everyone bringing him up all of a sudden? She'd never confided to anyone—not even Starli or Toni—about her favorite dream. A dark haired man, tall, and strong, who drove a fast white car, who just happened to stop at Undiscovered Treasures. He would see her, and they would fall in love forever and ever.

First Toni, and now Toby trying to throw her at Andy. He'd been in her life forever, almost like a brother, and he'd always had a hangdog look around her. In turns, she'd followed, teased, put up with, ignored, and then scorned the boy-turned man. But it hadn't affected Andy's devotion to her.

Too bad. She wanted more than an ordinary guy who wasn't passionate about anything but his paintings. Someone who was glamorous and different.

She'd hang on to her dream.

Chapter Five

Four hours after Toby left, Caro stood with arms akimbo surveying her work. She'd finished the huge storage room where they kept their antiques, collectibles, and junk. Each item sparkled, or at least was polished as highly as she could get it. The room oozed a piney scent from the cleaner she'd used on the floor.

Now what? She needed something else to keep her busy all evening. She hated to admit it, but the empty apartment upstairs had lost its appeal for her. Once in awhile, she relished having the whole apartment to herself. She'd choose a good book, her favorite CD, and soak in a tub of bubbly water.

Unfortunately, tonight wasn't turning out to be one of those. She was itchy with wanting something and had no clue what it was.

Earlier she'd thought she'd begin her investigating, but a slew of early afternoon customers had kept her busy up till closing time. The storage room had taunted her until she'd given in and finished it.

Now the thought of assuming the job of detective was anything but attractive. She just didn't *feel* like it.

She rambled about the shop and breathed in deeply. Musty books and glowing old-fashion lamps. Carved chests and bottles of all colors. She stopped beside the antique music box, wound it, and watched the tiny ballerina twirl around and around.

Just like her life. Always spinning around and going nowhere. She loved Toby and her best friends, Starli and Toni. She loved UT, but her life revolved around everything but *her*. Why wasn't her life about *her*?

How was her life going to change if she didn't take things into her own hands? If she wanted a man, she'd better get out there and find one.

The ringing of the phone interrupted her thoughts. Toby, no doubt, checking up on her. He'd probably sensed she really was depressed. He was that way.

"Caroline?"

Andy?

"Have you plans for tonight?"

"I've been working."

A pause. Then he spoke again in a quiet voice. "Would you like to go to the high school drama tonight?"

"With you?" Yikes. That was blunt. Caro bit her lip. She had planned on going, but had forgotten all about it. Blake, Toni's stepson, had a bit part in it.

"Unless you had plans to go with someone else?"

Couldn't the man ever get riled up? Caro clenched the phone receiver. "I don't have time to get ready. Besides I need to finish the work here."

"It doesn't start until eight."

Caro's gaze shot to the cat clock on the wall, with its constant, swinging tail. Six-thirty.

Andy's voice took on a coaxing edge. "Toni and Perrin are going. I told them to save seats for us."

"You took for granted I'd go?"

"I hoped you'd want to go." Andy countered in that patient voice of his.

Eureka. Couldn't he ever show doubt or anger or something?

"They're putting on *My Fair Lady,*" Toby added.

Ooh. He knew she loved that show. Was he trying to bribe her? Her defenses weakened. She really didn't have to finish any more cleaning tonight. She didn't even want to. Her spirits jumped at the thought of seeing the kids put on the play. Fun for the evening. Toni and Perrin would no doubt want to stop for a snack or even invite them back to their home.

She caved. "Okay. I'll go."

Pleasure warmed Andy's voice, and she could just imagine his mouth widening. "Wonderful. I'll pick you up at 7:30."

Depression gone, Caro sped for her room on the second floor. She'd planned on cleaning their apartment, but no time for that now. She wanted a bathtub soak.

~*~

When the doorbell rang, Caro clambered down the stairs, then stopped to catch her breath before opening the door. Her stomach lurched with sudden nervousness. What? It was Andy, after all. Not a date. And not her prince.

Andy's lips tipped up a little and his eyes shone with delight. His gaze fell to her outfit, then rose to meet her eyes again.

An irrepressible desire to glance down at her clothes ate at her. Was she not okay? But before she had time to squash the idea, he held out a flat package.

"What's this?" Caro stared at the brown paper-wrapped object.

He shook his head. "Open it."

She turned away, then threw over her shoulder. "Come on in."

The string slid loose when she pulled on the end. She shoved the paper away and stared down at the picture in front of her, then looked up at Andy. It was a double image of Eliza from *My Fair Lady*, showing her going from rags to riches.

"It's the loveliest picture I've ever seen. Where did you find it?"

Andy pointed at the right hand bottom corner.

Surprise rippled through her. "You? You painted this?"

"A little different than my usual work, but I promised the high school to do a few posters for them to sell. Did this in some spare time. Didn't turn out too badly. I think." He eyed the painting.

"It's the best thing you've ever done." Caro gushed and lifted the picture.

"If you say so. But I knew how much you loved this show. Thought you might as well have a memento. Sell it if you don't want it."

The light in his eyes warmed her heart. Caro clutched it to her chest. "I'll never sell it. I love it. Thank you."

"We'd better go if we're going to get there on time."

Caro set her picture on the counter. She cast a last loving look at the piece of beauty, then preceded Andy out the door.

She'd never been tongue-tied in her life, but the ten-minute ride to the high school lasted forever. After that amazing gift, she should have been chattering like a blue jay. What to talk about? Caro scrambled in her mind for something, anything to say.

"Why don't you paint like this all the time?" She asked, then wished she'd bitten her tongue. Why bring up a touchy subject? Andy knew she did not like his works. Caro slid a corner-eyed glance at him. He wasn't too much taller than she, and lean, but the muscles on his body kept him from being too thin. He generally worked in tatty jeans and sweatshirts or tees, but they suited him. And anyway she was used to seeing him in his work clothes.

Tonight though he sported a white oxford shirt and pressed khakis. Her gaze went to his hands. He'd worked on them, for only a tiny smudge of paint around his nails gave away his career. No matter how he tried, he'd never get all the paint off those nice hands of his.

What on earth was the matter with her tonight?

"Why are you smiling like a mischievous cat?"

"You can't get rid of the evidence no matter what you do, can you?" She looked at his hands gripping the bug's steering wheel.

He lifted one and pulled a wry expression, one side of his lips tilting up. "I scrubbed these things three times. That's the price I pay for working with oils."

"Don't worry about it." Caro brushed at the strands of hair tickling her neck. "I like them like that."

For a second a glint of something blazed from his eyes, then his gaze was back on the street. "Do you realize that's the first nice thing you've said—from your heart—to me in years?"

Did he think she was cozying up to him? Oh, dear, why had she come? She'd better steer the conversation back to something safe.

Back? There hadn't been much of a conversation. She looked out her passenger window in a desperate search for *some*thing to talk about when she realized Andy had turned into the high school parking lot.

At last.

They weeded their way through the ambling parents and chattering kids. Toni stood on the school steps and waved when she saw them. She gave both of them a quick hug. "Perrin's saving our seats. We've got front row."

"How did you manage that?" Caro looped her arm through Toni's, and they waltzed through the door together.

"Perrin donated money for the set. Isn't he the greatest? He was one of the ones with first choice on seats."

"Figures." Caro pulled a moue. "I heard Blake's a really good actor."

"He is. We're so proud of him. He's only playing a bit part this year, but his teacher said, next year, he'd for sure have a more important role." Toni swerved past a couple blocking the aisle.

After they'd settled in their seats, Caro turned to her friend, "Have you heard anything from Starli and Joel?"

"No, but they were in Scotland this week. She'll call soon."

The play started, and Caro's attention riveted on the amateur actors. Once again, the plot swept her into the action. Her heart pounded with emotion as the beautiful story unfolded. The first act ended, and the audience erupted into applause.

As Caro and her friends stood to head for the restrooms, Caro caught sight of Andy's neighbors, the Nortons. She hesitated when she remembered Andy's missing paintings. Now would be a good time to talk with them.

Toni glanced back at her over her shoulder. "Coming?"

"Go ahead. I want to speak to someone." She waved her friend and Perrin away and headed toward the couple.

She'd almost reached them when she realized someone was following her. She stopped and turned. Andy bumped into her.

"What are you doing?" She narrowed her eyes.

"Going with you—wherever that is."

His assurance irked her. Did he think she wanted him following her like a tail on a kite? "I'm just going to talk with the Nortons. You don't have to go." Caro wanted him to go away. She didn't want to ask her inexperienced questions in front of him.

"I won't get in your way." Andy held up both hands, palms toward her, and Caro saw a sudden stubbornness illuminated in his usually warm brown eyes.

Feeling like she'd been attacked with puppy-dog syndrome, she gave up and trotted the rest of the way.

"Hey, you guys. How're you doing?"

Sharen and Bob Norton, in their thirties and active in Caro's church, gave her and Andy a hug. "The kids are doing great, aren't they?"

Caro knew their two twin daughters had a part in the play tonight. "Sydney and Sierra are perfect for their parts. I predict they've got a fantastic future ahead of them."

Sharen laughed and cast her husband a sideways glance. "Just what I keep telling Bob. He seems to think they need to plan on a more stable career."

"They'll find their way eventually." Caro shrugged. When she heard Bob ask Andy about his painting, she darted into the conversation with her own question.

"Have either of you seen anyone strange around Andy's place?"

"Sure. All the time." Bob guffawed. "You never know when someone will stop in after one of this guy's paintings. He keeps on, and he'll be as famous as Picasso."

"Well, that would be nice, but can't see it happening." Andy's mouth twisted in a wry grin. "I'm afraid not everyone takes to my art."

Was he talking about her? She could *feel* his gaze studying her.

"They need their heads examined then. You're good." Bob slapped the slighter man on the shoulder.

He liked Andy's work, too? Caro harrumphed to herself. Comparing that stuff to Picasso. He didn't seem like the type to know art. Showed what Bob Norton knew about it.

"Well, someone's stolen two of his paintings." What else was there to ask these two? Caro scratched her head mentally. "Either one of you know anyone who's in the market for stolen works?"

Both of them shook their heads, but had Bob dropped his eyes?

"Not us, but if we hear anything, we'll let you know."

Andy took her arm as they walked back to their seats. "Good job."

"Yeah, right." Caro snorted. What did he know?

"There wasn't much to ask. You'll think of more with the next ones."

Caro ignored him and sank in her seat beside Toni.

"Where'd you go?"

"Went to speak to the Nortons. Wanted to find out if they'd seen anything suspicious around Andy's place."

Perrin leaned forward. "What's going on?"

"He had a couple paintings stolen." Caro still couldn't believe anyone would want to steal such ugly work.

"Really? Didn't you tell us you'd been commissioned by Regency's?" Her pleasure for him shone in Toni's brown eyes.

"Three paintings a year for five years. Then an option to renew the contract if the paintings sell well."

"You're on your way to fame."

"You know what they say. If you don't enjoy what you do for a living, you're in the wrong business. Thank God, I'm doing what I love to do and have God's blessing too. What more could I ask?" Andy glanced at Caro.

What was that glance about?

"I've been wanting to ask you to do a portrait of Toni. Would you be interested?" Perrin asked in a low voice as the lights in the house blinked once, twice, a signal the play was about to begin again.

"Perrin, Andy won't have time to do a picture of me." Toni's laughing protest sent color to her cheeks.

A woman in love.

"Sure. I'll *make* time for you two." Andy patted Toni on the hand.

The empty stage up front was ready to lighten with action and color again, but a sudden ambiguity of feelings swept over her. What was wrong with her? She couldn't understand this mixed up feeling inside of her. She was with her dearest friends, except for Andy, of course, and really he wasn't that bad.

Not that she'd ever admit it out loud.

Then why the fierce longing banging deep within her chest? A breath escaped her lips when the auditorium went dark.

Something bothered her about Bob Norton. His eyes had dropped too quickly. Almost as if he was evading her questions. Or maybe thinking up an answer. Did he know more than he was telling?

Although not bosom buddies, she'd always liked the Nortons. Besides their activity in the church, he was a successful businessman in town, and a staunch supporter of the school system. In fact, if she remembered correctly, he'd been voted in as a school board member last term. He'd always been hailed as a friendly sort.

Was he too back-slapping friendly? Was there more to Bob Norton than met the eye?

A kaleidoscope of thoughts whirled in her mind. When a strand of hair brushed against her cheek, she forced herself to focus on the surroundings and sensed Andy's stare at her.

She blinked and whispered. "What?"

He leaned closer. She could see his white teeth gleaming from the glare of the stage lights. "Enjoying the play?"

Caro swept a glance at the stage and realized they were just minutes from ending. Where had she been?

"Loving it." She would not let him know her mind had wandered away.

"So much that you've not seen any of this act."

The words were so low Caro doubted her ears. Had Andy just whispered he knew she wasn't paying attention? How could he know? Her gaze had been fastened to the stage.

She cast him a swift glance, then concentrated on the last remaining minutes. When the whole auditorium-filled family and friends stood at the end and clapped, Caro joined in.

Toni turned to Caro and Andy. "Perrin and I are stopping at The Mountain View for dessert and coffee. Are you coming? Our treat."

Before Caro could respond, Andy nodded. "We'll be there with bells on."

He was taking her acceptance for granted. Again. Caro snapped. "Can't you think of a better analogy?"

For just an instant something flickered in

Andy's eyes. Anger? No way. She'd never seen him angry, not even the time in high school when she'd accidentally spilled soda over a carefully painted picture of his for art class. Not even in all the years she'd ignored his advances.

Caro fumbled with her coat, but Andy's hands reached for it. Heat scorched her cheeks. Why did she have to be so hateful around this gentle man? She *didn't* have to. Laying a hand on his arm, she croaked the apology from her throat. "Sorry."

He threw an arm around her as they joggled their way through the crowd. "No problem. You're right, I should have thought of something interesting and daring. I'll try to be more inventive when I'm around you from now on."

In spite of Andy's soothing words, misery railed up inside her. She wanted to cringe. She'd seen his eyes when she'd slashed at him.

Had that been sadness deep within them?

Chapter Six

As Andy closed her door, she watched him cross in front of his beat up vehicle, and her heart softened.

He was a good man and her brother's best friend. Surely that counted for something. No more grouchy moods. They made her feel too guilty. It didn't matter what his artwork was like. She'd make nice or die trying. And as far as his devotion was concerned, she'd just have to learn to be more adept at dodging it.

He stopped before getting in the car and dug his phone from his pocket. He listened for a minute, and even in the car with the windows up, Caro could hear the note of disturbance in his voice.

When he finally hung up, he stood silently, his fingers tapping a little on the top of the car.

She leaned over and spoke his name, and he moved to get in the car.

After Andy started his car, Caro twisted in her seat. "What are you working on now?"

"Meaning my painting?" He steered out of the parking lot. "You really want to know or are you just being nice?"

A painter he might not be, but he was astute at reading her. "Of course, I want to know. Why else would I ask?"

"Like I said, trying to be polite." He gave her a quick grin before turning back to his driving.

"I've begun one of the works Regency's contracted."

"What is it?"

"It's a street scene. If you really want to see it, I'll show you sometime."

That sounded interesting. There wasn't any way he could paint *that* picture depressingly, could he? Caro shook her head as she watched Andy park his wreck of a car between two Cadillacs. He didn't appear to notice, because he opened his door and stepped out as if he hadn't a care in the world.

She threw open her own door and started to get out, caught her foot and sprawled on the pavement. She looked up as Andy rushed to her side.

"Are you okay?" He knelt beside her, his voice raspy. "Did you hurt your hand?"

Her whole left palm was skinned and oozed blood. At least she hadn't broken it when she fell on it. Worse, she'd ripped the sleeve of her blouse. "I guess that does it. I can't go in here looking like this."

Andy took her hand, lifted her up, and helped her sit back on the passenger seat. "I've got a first aid kit in my glove compartment. Let me look at it."

Caro bit her lip as Andy washed the scraped skin and applied first ointment, then bandages to her hand. His fingers were so strong, yet gentle, and somehow knowing Andy was working on her cuts soothed the pain.

When he'd put away the kit, he stared down at her. He propped his chin on a fist. "I'm not sure, but I think I could...Can you stand for a minute?"

Silently, she did as he asked.

"May I?"

She shrugged. What could it hurt?

"I think I've got some pins here somewhere. Hold on, I think we can do something with your sleeve." Andy rummaged again through his glove compartment, then straightened. He went to work and in minutes he'd finished.

Caro lifted her arm. The material fluttered. How had he done it? "What did you do to it?"

Andy's face reddened. "Nothing much. Cut most of it off and pleated the rest here and there. You really ought to do the same with the other one so they match."

"Why not? Have a go at it."

"Sure you trust me? It might turn into a worse disaster." His brows pulled together as if he wasn't quite sure whether to believe her or not.

"Don't worry about it."

Once he'd finished, Caro studied his work, flapped her arms to watch the thin organza material flutter. "I like it."

"Now you're on top of fashion."

"Are you sure?" Caro repeated his earlier question, but wondered how put together she looked, then glanced up at the man beside her. "Sure they won't throw me out?"

Andy closed the tin holding his pins and tossed it inside his car. He reached for her hand. "Don't worry. You look fantastic."

She couldn't understand it. She walked beside him, her hand tucked in the crook of his arm and did feel fantastic, bandages, repaired clothes, and all. She shook her head. She must have that appendage in the proverbial clouds.

"Where did you learn to do that kind of stuff?"

"Meaning clothes repair?" Andy grinned. "In college, I took a few courses in creative clothes design. Thought at one time I might major in that, but my love for oils prevailed."

"You're a multi-faceted person." Caro couldn't stop the admiring glance.

Toni saw them coming and said something to Perrin, who turned and motioned to them.

As Caro and Andy walked up to them, a tiny frown grew on Toni's forehead. She cocked her head and studied her friend. "Did you go home and change? You look different."

"Better?" Caro shared a glance with Andy and wanted to laugh.

"I didn't say that, but you're different."

Just then the maître d' approached, led them to their table, and nothing more was said.

After they placed their orders, Perrin sat back. "Andy, tell us more about your contract with Regency's. What do they want from you?"

"My usual style. When my agent approached them, I guess they were pretty impressed." Andy glanced at Caro. "They happened to have some important clients there at the time, and one of them gave a down payment for one right then."

"That's pretty impressive." Toni's eyes sparkled. "Congratulations."

"It is exciting. It's like at last I'm going somewhere."

"The way I've been hearing it, you're getting known in some wide areas. The last time I was in Chicago, a friend of mine was on the phone with his attorney allocating money for the purchase of a Carrington painting. If I understood right, he was trying to outbid someone else."

Caro couldn't believe it. Two people bidding for one of those gloomy works? "Are you sure it was our Andy?"

Three heads turned in her direction. Ergh. Why hadn't she kept her opinion to herself?

"I just meant..." What had she meant? "I mean, Andy's not done too much advertising. How could someone clear over in Chicago have seen one of his paintings?"

Feeble. She could see the bemused expression on Andy's face. No doubt he knew exactly what she'd meant.

"I have my agent to thank—and God, of course, for any progress I've made in sales. And Stephanie's been a blessing."

"Why haven't we had a chance to meet this wonder woman yet?" Toni's eyes sparkled with interest.

"She's only been with me for a month or little less."

Andy stretched his arm along the back of Caro's seat, and instantly she leaned forward.

"Funny thing is, I keep thinking I've seen her somewhere, but for the life of me, I can't remember where. She insists we haven't met. I'm just glad she's working for me now."

"Anything to give you more time to paint. I'm happy for you, Andy. But back to your art. What I like about them is their depth. I search my soul every time I see one of your new ones." Toni's voice took on a subdued, almost holy, ring to it.

"The strength. I like the power they evoke. Lots of men relate to them." Perrin picked up his cup of coffee the waitress set down.

Bor-i-n-g. Caro yawned and let her mind drift from the conversation. Her gaze wandered about The Mountain View Inn. Her gaze rested on first one customer than another. Then she looked again. Was that guy staring at her? No way. He was probably looking at Toni and hoping Perrin was her date and not a husband.

He was good-looking in a hollywood-ish way. What was he doing in a small town like Appleton? For that matter, what was he doing in West Virginia—if he was from Hollywood?

Caro leaned to her left, and the guy leaned the same direction. He *was* looking at her. She moaned, dropped her gaze and struggled to keep from blushing.

"What on earth are you doing?" Toni's voice interrupted her musings.

"Is your hand hurting? Need some pain medicine?" Andy's forehead creased with concern.

Had she moaned out loud? Caro's glance shot across the room, but the guy had risen with his companions, and they were strolling away. Too bad.

"Caro?"

"Sorry, I was thinking." And musing about a man she didn't know.

"I thought I heard you moan. Are you okay?" Toni's smooth brow wrinkled.

"I'm fine. Don't pay any attention to me."

The conversation swirled on, and Caro tried to put herself into it. No use mooning over what wasn't to be.

But something in Andy's tone caught her attention, and she focused on what he was saying.

"Detective Eddie is there and said he'd wait till I got home."

"I'm sorry, I was daydreaming again. Why is Eddie there? What happened?"

Andy rubbed his forehead as if trying to wipe away a beginning headache. "Someone broke into my studio again—tonight and stole another painting. Or at least, Stephanie thinks one is gone."

"Oh, Andy, I'm so sorry. Can we do anything?" Toni's concerned voice begged to help.

"I can't think of a thing right now, Toni, but thanks. I hate to break up our good time, but I really should go and find out what's missing. I hope it's not the painting I finished this morning for Regency's."

Andy and Caro headed toward his car and waved as Perrin and Toni passed them in her bright red mustang.

Andy swung open her door.

"Toni adores her car." Caro looked up at Andy. In the streetlight, his jaw seemed firmer than usual, his body more intense. Where was the passive image she always carried of him?

Andy nodded as he stood by the car door, his gaze fastened on the tail lights of the sports car. "She'll be a pleasure to paint. Capturing the gentleness will be a challenge."

Caro couldn't deny Toni's personality. Everyone in Appleton knew Toni found something good in every one she met.

The best she could hope for herself was a comment of her clumsiness. Some might even go so far as to call her loyal. That was something, wasn't it? Caro huffed out a breath of air.

Andy got in on the driver's side and turned the key. When nothing happened, he looked puzzled, then resigned. “Can anything else happen tonight?”

“What's wrong?” Was the battery dead? Was he out of gas?

“I don't know. I just bought a new battery last week.” Andy swung open his door and went around the back to open the trunk.

Caro twisted in her seat to watch. Andy fiddled with something in the engine. She swung her own door open and hurried to join him.

“Can I do anything?”

“Mind getting my flashlight in the glove compartment?”

Caro got the flashlight and returned to hold it for him while Andy checked the battery terminals. Their heads almost touched as both leaned under the hood. A voice behind them spoke.

“Are you having trouble? Need some help?”

Caro jumped, bumped her head on the trunk lid and lifted a hand to rub at the smarting spot. She turned, ready to frown at the inconsiderate person.

The Hollywood man she'd seen inside the restaurant stood there.

Was this guy good-looking or what? Caro patted her chest before she could stop herself. She opened her mouth to answer, but Andy beat her to it.

"Can't quite figure out what the problem is. Since this is a new battery, it should be okay." Andy rubbed a grease-smeared hand across one cheek, leaving him with a Wild West look of a Native American ready for battle.

A giggle exploded from her before she could hold it back. She swung her gaze between the two men. The stranger's black hair shone, his eyes were brown, almost black—darker than Andy's honey brown ones—amused, yet not unkind. There was the tiniest of scars beside his mouth that didn't distract one iota from his good looks. He was her dream come true.

Her gaze swept to Andy's smudged face. His shirtsleeve already held a grimy spot where he'd brushed up against the engine. His tawny hair stood on end.

Whereas the new guy towered over her, Andy was just inches taller, not too tall nor too short.

Hollywood Guy shrugged. "Sorry, I know nothing about cars. But I can give you a lift home. By the way, I'm Lincoln Tillis, but my friends call me Linc."

Andy extended a hand, drew it back, and reached for a rag to wipe his hands. "Sorry. It's good to meet you, Linc. This is Caroline Gibson, and I'm Andy Carrington."

"Glad to meet you." Linc's nod was full of pleasure, but his gaze was on her. "I've heard about you."

Caro blinked. "You have?"

"You're quite famous in certain circles." The mischievous look in Linc's eyes told Caro he knew something she didn't.

"I am?" *Brilliant. Caro Gibson, can't you come up with something more interesting?*

"Forgive me. You caught my attention in the restaurant. You have an expressive face."

Really?

"I thought you must be the Caroline Gibson everyone at my church is talking about. Actually, I've seen your picture."

"You have?"

"I'm from High Hill Community Church in Clarksburg. We used your plays in our Christmas pageant the last two years. That's one of the reasons I'm here. Could I persuade you to write another one with specific details just for us?"

"Are you serious?"

"We're very serious. We'll pay you well."

Her simple little plays? At Starli's insistence she needed to expand, she'd had fliers made up, placed a few advertisements in magazines and newsletters, and advertised on Undiscovered Treasures' website. Granted, she'd done well for a small-time playwright and even started selling a few outside of West Virginia.

But famous? Her?

"She is the best comedy playwright I've read in a long time. Especially when you see the meaningfulness woven below the surface of the comedy routines."

Caro knew her mouth had flown open, then her eyes narrowed. Was he making up to her to gain her attention?

"That's the feedback we've gotten." Linc's voice was enthusiastic. "Our attendance doubled last year when it got out we were using one of the Caroline Gibson plays again."

"Th-anks." She wanted to bite her lip at the stutter, but she was so thrilled her insides were jumping like playful kangaroos.

Linc turned to Andy. "So can I give you folks a lift?"

Andy tossed the rag he'd used onto the engine and slammed the trunk. "I'd appreciate that. I'll call and have the garage tow it tomorrow."

When they pulled up in front of Undiscovered Treasures, both men swung open their doors to help her out.

Nice. I might get spoiled if this happens much. She sighed as she watched the tall driver stride around the front of his black SUV. Fat chance she had.

It was Andy who opened her door, but after climbing out, it was Linc who faced her.

"Is this your business?" Linc's eyes studied the building, then the sign. "'Rare entities for your personal expansion, antiques for your emotional depth, and junk for your funny bones!' Cute. I have to make a quick run home, but I could stop by in two, maybe three, days to discuss the play."

"Sure. I'd love to see—talk with you about it." Oops. Had she almost said, 'you?'"

"Good. Here, let me walk you to your door." Linc offered, but Andy's hand propelled her toward the building as he called back.

"I'll see to it. Be back in a jiffy."

"What are you doing?" Caro jerked her arm away. "You didn't have to be so—so impolite to him."

"You're my date. I'll see you to the door."

"Tonight wasn't a date. We're just friends who went to a play together." Caro glanced at the man beside her. His firmed lips and stony face told her he was determined to have his way. "I'm just saying, it was awfully nice of him to bring us home. He doesn't even know us."

The shrug he gave her told her he wasn't impressed. "Anyone would have done the same."

Frustration spurted through her. "We wouldn't have needed a ride if you kept that piece of junk in shape."

They reached the door, and Andy took the keys from her and unlocked the door. "I suppose you like SUV's better?"

Andy was being bullheaded for no reason. After all, Linc could be a good customer for her. Caro ignored the niggling excitement that maybe—maybe he could be more.

"As a matter of fact, I adore SUV's." Her gaze went to the man leaning against the big vehicle. Could he hear them arguing?

"I hope your painting is okay. Let me know, will you?" She lowered her voice. "Thanks for the evening, Andy. Good-bye."

"Wait a minute. You don't know this man. He could be married, an ex-con, or..."

He was ignoring her statement of diplomacy. As if her concern for this new problem and her thanks meant nothing. "Or what? He's a prospective customer."

"I saw the look in your eyes. The same one I've seen a hundred—no, a thousand—times. Your head's in the clouds. You're dreaming."

"Since when is it wrong to dream?" Caro tilted her head, but, again, her gaze sought the figure at the end of the sidewalk.

Andy's hand touched hers tentatively, but the look in his eyes unsettled her.

"It's never wrong to dream, Caroline, never. Just make sure you're dreaming for the right thing."

She wanted to jerk her gaze from his, but couldn't.

"And to really love a woman, a man has to know her dreams." His voice barely reached her ears, but Caro felt her eyes widening. He was singing a message to her. Did he think he knew what her dreams were? Then he'd be disappointed.

With a squeeze of her hand, he trotted back to the waiting sports car and the man who drove it.

The taillights winked at her as it turned the corner. Signaling her a promise of a return with the handsome man in tow? Caro looked up at the star lit sky. She'd waited long enough. It was time to shake the reins a little. "A girl's gotta do what a girl's gotta do, doesn't she, Lord?"

Nodding, she shut the door and locked it. It was definitely time to put feet to her prayers.

In three days, she'd see Linc again. It couldn't come too soon to suit her.

Chapter Seven

The bedside clock read 5:17 a.m. when Caro rolled out of bed three mornings later. She didn't have to shake herself awake today. Her nerves were jumping with anticipation.

What to wear? Casual? Business? She dithered twenty minutes, trying on and discarding seven outfits.

She picked up a white shirt. No. White washed out her complexion.

The tie-dyed was too...undignified, especially for a famous playwright.

She frowned at her reflection in the mirror. "You don't have the least idea what looks good on you."

A nagging sensation of inferiority echoed repeatedly down deep inside herself. She eyed the not blond, not brown hair, and wished for the millionth time she had curly hair like Toni's or stunning blond hair like Starli's.

She rubbed at the freckles scattered across her nose, then sucked in her wide mouth to make it smaller. In spite of the fact that Starli called her freckles adorable, and Toni said her mouth gave her character, she despised both.

No use. She wasn't going to change her looks no matter what she did.

In a second, her eyes twinkled back at herself. "Okay. So what?"

She pulled on her favorite jean outfit, tucked in the soft blue shirt material, and swiped a brush through her hair.

"Come on, Angel, let's go have breakfast." Her white cat curled around her ankles in answer and followed her to the tiny kitchen area.

She shook out Kitty Nibbles, tossed on top of the cat food a bite or two of sliced turkey—the same turkey she hid from Toby knowing he'd devour it all, leaving none for poor Angel—then studied the shelf, one finger tapping her lips.

"Hm-m-m. Chocolate or strawberry pop tarts?"

Angel lifted her head and smacked her lips as she stared at her. She blinked, then dug into her breakfast again as if saying, "Don't bother me. I've got important stuff here to take care of."

After carrying two of the warmed strawberry tarts downstairs to the shop, she poured a huge cup of coffee. What she did want so dearly she could taste it, was a cappuccino. That was out. She had work to do and no time to run to The Coffee House after one.

She hitched herself on top of a barstool and pulled her pad and a pencil close. Now to work while she waited on customers.

She had no idea what kind of play the High Hill Church would want. Something specific, but it wouldn't hurt to get some new ideas in her head.

Hmmm. She sipped her warmed up coffee from last night as she thought. What about...a clown? Maybe a setting in early 1900. A circus? A clown in study who'd run away from his home life seeking fun and adventure?

Possibly. But clowns were kind of creepy. Caro shivered.

What about a returning-home-on-leave soldier? Stories about the armed forces were popular right now. Maybe he's injured? Confused? Disheartened? No, that theme had been overused. How about a reversal? He comes home and finds his family in turmoil, their faith wavering, and he has to deal with it.

Not too bad. Might work.

The phone rang, and Caro swept it up.

"What's going on, Sis?"

"Hey, Toby. When you coming back?"

She heard his chuckle.

"I've only been gone a couple days. Surely you don't miss me already?"

"Well, if I have to be brutally honest—I don't want you returning too soon and ruining my plans."

"What kind of plans?"

She could imagine his nose quivering in interest. Ha. Let him stew in juices of his own making.

"Never mind. It's not your concern," She spoke as loftily as she could, choking back the giggle.

A brief silence. "Wondering how you and ol' Andy are doing on his lost paintings?"

She'd totally forgotten about them. "Uh, I talked to some people."

"You and Andy went to *My Fair Lady*?"

"Yes. The kids did a fantastic job. We met Toni and Perrin for the play and afterwards went for a snack."

"Andy mentioned that. Said he had trouble with his bug."

"He called you?"

"I called this morning to talk with him about business. I'm glad you two had a fun date."

Her temper edged up a notch. "Date? Why does everyone insist on calling it a date? It wasn't exactly a world-class event. I was planning on going anyway. We just went together. No big deal."

"Take it easy." Silence, then Toby went on. "Remember the gorgeous red-head in town?"

Had everyone in this town met this creature, but her? Caro jerked the phone from her ear and eyed it. Serve him right if she hung up on him. "I haven't laid eyes on this paragon yet."

"Do I hear a bit of peevishness?"

Toby was such a nuisance. One she loved, but still a nuisance.

He went on as if totally unaware—which she knew wasn't true—of his irritating digs at her. "A total knock-out, the way I heard it."

Is that what he called to talk about? "Can we ch—?"

"She's in town for a reason, I think."

"What makes you say that?" Her interest piqued. "Toni said she's a daughter of someone important from New York."

Toby snickered. "Yeah, I guess. But there's another reason. Something to do with Andy—maybe his paintings."

"Probably work related." Caro sniffed.

"Could be, but maybe not either. Andy's going places."

What was that supposed to mean?

"He said you guys met a man from one of

the bigger churches in Clarksburg wanting you to write a special play for them. Sounds interesting."

Really? Did Andy have to tell all her news? "Yeah, it does. He's a very attract—nice person."

Was Toby hesitating? Uh oh, advice coming.

"At the risk of repeating myself, take it easy. Don't throw yourself at him."

Ergh. "I've never in my life thrown myself at any man, Toby Gibson. I can't believe you said that."

"No, you haven't. But what I'm talking about is letting your heart rule your head. Don't fall for this guy unless you know he reciprocates the feeling. You do seem to fall for the wrong guys, Caro."

"Since when have I asked you for advice in my life?" Caro slammed the phone down, then repented. Toby was being protective.

She sighed. The old fashion bell above the door tinkled as the door flew open. Andy walked in carrying two large cups. "Hey, Caroline. Had to come into town. Stopped at the Coffee House and got us a cappuccino."

She wanted to snap at him, tell him she was busy, to get lost, anything to relieve some of the pressure building inside, but the tempting aroma wafting from the cup convinced her to change her mind. She reached for hers and took a cautious sip. "Delicious. Thanks."

Andy settled on the second bar stool, and Caro eyed him. Was he settled in for the day?

"What'd you come into town for?" *To see cute Red-Head?*

"Had to pick up some paint supplies from

the post office."

"Oh, yeah?" Very convenient excuse to stop by. Caro dropped that thought. There wasn't anything unusual about him stopping by, but usually Toby was here. She'd always blamed his frequent visits on their friendship.

"Thought we could work on my missing paintings this morning." Andy picked up his own cappuccino. "I've got some free time."

"Shouldn't you be painting? Don't you have some contracts to fulfill?"

"Yes, I should be painting, as my thief did steal another painting the other night. Now I'm back to square one. I've got a good start on it and hope to finish it next week." He shifted on his seat. "So I'm taking the morning off to go detecting with you—if you want."

"I wondered, but since I hadn't heard, thought maybe it was a false alarm. Sorry, Andy. Very sorry." She touched his hand. "What did you have in mind?"

"Thought we could talk to some of the neighbors and maybe the sheriff?"

A glance down at her notepad reminded her of Linc's planned visit today. "I can't. I've got—uh, plans today."

"Linc?" Andy's brow shot up. "When's he coming?"

"He didn't say." Why hadn't he given her some idea of when he'd be here? It'd be lovely to work on the mystery.

"You're going to sit here waiting all day on him?"

Why did he have to make it sound like the most unpleasant thing in the world?

"I happen to love working in my shop. I

guess I can wait for Linc while doing something I love."

The man beside her didn't argue. He stood, picked up his cup, and headed toward the door. "Makes sense. I can probably get Steph or someone to help me look around a bit. Need to get this figured out so I can quit worrying it might happen again."

What? Andy was going to get that...kid to help him solve his mystery? She sniffed. He'd forgotten about her quickly enough. "Wait. I could probably leave a note on the door for Linc. I shouldn't be away from the shop more than an hour."

Andy turned, his face beaming. "Great. Let's get a move on."

A glance at the clothes she had on, then Caro jumped from her perch. She scribbled a note, grabbed the roll of tape, and slapped the paper to the door as they left.

~*~

She stopped at the sight of his faded blue car parked close, and he almost plowed into her again.

"You got it fixed already?"

"Would you believe? Terminals were bad. Ted replaced them in no time, and I headed over here." Andy opened the passenger door and waited till Caroline slid in. As he hurried around to his side, he glanced back down the street. No sign of Linc yet. Good. Maybe he could get her away before Big Town Boy got here.

The engine started on the first try, but as Andy turned the corner, he caught a glimpse in the rearview mirror of the black SUV a block behind.

Just in the nick of time. He couldn't have stopped his grin for any amount of money. *Thank you, God.* "Where shall we go first?"

A tiny frown spread between her brows. "Think we can find Jeffrey now? Maybe he's seen something."

"Don't know, but we can give it a shot."

They drove twenty minutes before seeing Jeffrey pulled under the shade of a big maple.

"Eating lunch."

"And examining the mail, looks like."

Her voice was a shade too dry, and Andy wanted to chuckle. Everyone knew how nosy Jeffrey, the postman was, but he was friendly and likeable, so most on his route ignored his least desirable trait.

They swung open the car doors at the same time as he dropped the letters he held in one hand, close to his mail bag.

The mail man held up a whole-wheat sandwich and called out, "Lunch. I'd offer you some, but I've only got one sandwich, and I'm not much in the mood to share. What's up, you two?"

"We wondered if we could talk with you about those paintings of Andy's." Caro nodded at the man squatted beside the door.

"Okay. Not sure I know much though. What do you want to know?" Jeffrey took another bite of his sandwich.

"Have you seen anyone in the past month hanging around Andy's place?"

"He's always got someone around wanting to see what he's painting."

"Right. But any one you didn't recognize? A

stranger, maybe? Suspicious acting person?"

"No. Wait. It wasn't suspicious. I only noticed the car because Mr. Bennett, your neighbor, was talking to whoever was in it. It was the first of the month I saw this sports car—" The man wrinkled his forehead.

"What color was it, Jeffrey?" Andy leaned back against the door of the mail vehicle to steady himself.

"Red. It was a Camaro. I remember now. Someday I'm gonna have one."

Andy grunted. Donald Snelling? He hadn't seen Donald since the first of the month, and his agent had said nothing about being in Appleton.

"What?" Caro shot him a glance.

"Sounds like my agent's car, but it can't be him." Andy shrugged. "He didn't stop by. Why else would he be in this area?"

"You didn't talk with him?"

"On the phone, but I assumed he was in New York." Andy stood and mock-punched Jeffrey's arm. "Thanks, I'll make sure you have a little extra something at Christmas."

He waved them away, and the two walked back to Andy's car. Caro stared at Andy over the roof of the small car. "If it wasn't him, then who could it have been?"

"Haven't the foggiest."

"Andy Carrington. You are the most irritating person." Caro climbed into the passenger seat and flopped against the back of the seat. "How can you cross someone off our list because you know them? Or worse, just want to think of them as innocent?"

He loved her like this, the freckles on her

upturned nose standing out when her cheeks flushed. "Sorry. Don't mean to. I just can't see how it could have been Donald. How many red Camaros around here do you suppose there are?"

"We should have asked Jeffrey if he noticed the license plate."

"Never thought of it." Andy snapped his fingers. "Exactly why I need your help. You think of the best things to ask."

"Yeah." She glanced down at her watch and sat up straighter. "It's been forty-five minutes. I've got to get back to the shop. Can't keep it closed all day. Besides, Linc may show up."

"Sure you don't want to talk to someone else first?" Andy started the car and pointed it back toward Undiscovered Treasures. He'd prefer driving straight out of town.

"Can't. You know Toby. He'll have my hide."

As much as he didn't want to admit it, she was right. She had an obligation to her business.

They had approached the middle of town, near the post office when Andy pointed. "There's Stephanie and Bob Norton."

"Where?"

"Over there, under the maple tree in front of the post office."

"I see them. Is she your assistant Stephanie? Who's the other man?" Caro leaned forward and stared out the side window.

"What other man? I'm driving, remember. I can't see him. The tree branches are hiding him."

"He's a big man, but I can't quite make out his features." Caro flopped against the back of the seat. “Go around the block.”

“Okay, but what are you thinking?”

“What is she holding?”

“I don't know. It looked like—”

“A big square flat package? About the size of one of your paintings, don't you think?”

“Didn’t notice.”

“Come on, Andy.”

“Are you saying you think Stephanie may be involved in theft?”

“Of course, I’m thinking theft. People who act suspicious get suspected.” The tiniest nibble of irritation ate its way up her stomach and into her voice. She motioned. “Pull over. I want to talk to them.”

Andy did as she asked.

But instead of jumping out, she dumped the contents from her shoulder bag into her lap and picked through the assortment. “I can't find it.”

“What are you looking for?”

Her face brightened at his question, and she held out her hand. “Let me see your cell. I must have forgotten mine at home again.”

“What on earth for?” He reluctantly handed it over.

She turned slightly and snapped several pictures of the three standing across the street then returned it to him. “Always wanted to subversively snap pictures of suspects. Figured this was the best opportunity I'd ever get.”

“Really, Caroline? We don't know they're suspects...”

She ignored him and swung her door open.

He followed her action but grabbed her arm. “Caro.”

When she looked at him over her shoulder, he urged. "I can't see my assistant stealing from me. Be careful what you say."

"Is she responsible for shipping your paintings?"

"Yes, and—"

"And did you order one shipped *today*?"

"You don't know that's what this is."

She gave him a look. "Stay here if you want. I'm going to talk with them."

"Just go easy on the accusation part."

"What do you take me for? I don't know your assistant, and she doesn't know me."

She called out to their church friend before reaching the couple. "Hi, Bob."

Andy sighed but followed. When Caro got a bug in her ear...

When had the third man disappeared? Andy gave a cautious look around but saw no one hurrying away as if trying to get as far from them as possible.

Bob turned, recognized them, and he gave them a wave. "Hey, you two. I didn't think you left your favorite hiding places unless an emergency insisted."

"Very funny, Bob."

He grinned and looked from Caro to Andy. "What *are* you guys doing in town on a weekday? Seriously, I know you both are usually busy with your businesses, especially during spring."

Had Stephanie's face turned a shade redder? She certainly appeared to be uncomfortable with the snap glances she aimed at him. Maybe she was playing hooky from the job and afraid Andy would fire her. Or maybe the flat cardboard package had something to do with her discomfort.

"We're still trying to find the person who took Andy's paintings. I wanted to ask you, Bob, if you saw a red Camaro earlier in the month hanging around Andy's property?"

"I'm not into cars much, Caro. As long as they take me where I want to go, I couldn't care less what they look like. What time frame are you talking?"

"I don't know. Do you know Andy's agent? What's his name again, Andy?"

So far, so good. Caroline could be a bit abrupt at times and not even realize she was bordering on insults. "Donald Snelling."

"As far as I know, I've never met him face to face."

Had Bob's eyes shifted away from Caroline's? Andy studied the man. He'd never had any trouble with any of his neighbors, had known most of them for years, and yet Bob definitely had the look of—what? Discomfort? Fear?

No. Surely not. Caroline's suspicions were making him suspect everyone too.

Caroline had turned her attention to his assistant. As hard as it'd been finding the one who suited him, he'd better pay attention to Caroline's questions. Annoying Stephanie was not what he wanted.

"Do you like working for Andy?"

Stephanie's eyes slanted sideways. When she saw Andy grinning, her body relaxed, and she nodded.

"It's the best job I've ever had, and I don't mean just the pay. I love the independence and variety. Most of all, Andy is great to work with."

Well. Kind of ruled out guilt on Stephanie's part. If she loved the job so much, she wouldn't want to jeopardize it, which was great news, as far as he was concerned. Regardless of the package in her hand. Perhaps it was something personal of hers.

Andy moved to leave, but Bob raised a hand.

"I wasn't going to say anything, because I really didn't think it was important enough to worry you over, Andy."

"Let Andy decide that, Bob."

"I don't know anything at all about Andy's missing pictures." Bob gave her a wry grin.

"Then?"

"The thirtieth of last month, I received a phone call. The person didn't identify himself."

"You didn't recognize his voice?"

"Pretty sure it was disguised someway. He wanted to know if I was up to giving your paintings a boost. When I asked him who he was, he ignored my question. When I asked him what he wanted me to do, he returned with vague replies. Nothing definite. Said if I was interested, he'd let me know later."

Bob swept him and Caro a glance. "Don't get me wrong. I want to see your career go and for you to make it big, but with nothing definite to work with, I didn't want to get involved."

"He said nothing else?" Weird. Could it have been Donald working his magic in a crazy way? Something he wanted to try but wasn't sure about yet?

"No. That's why I didn't want to say anything. It was all so vague, and I figured if the guy was on the up and up, why would he be so secretive?"

"Don't worry a thing about it. Sounds like a kook to me."

Andy clasped Caroline's arm, relief mixed with perplexity surging through him. He was glad Bob wasn't involved. Yet something strange was going on. How could someone think stealing Andy's paintings would advance his career?

The silence built up between them as they neared the shop. When Andy turned onto the lane and saw the black SUV, his heart flipped. He should have stayed away longer, regardless of obligations. Caroline's bright face did nothing for his mood, and when he pulled behind the waxed vehicle, she jumped out.

"Thanks, Andy. We'll work on your missing pictures again." Her voice floated behind her as she ran toward the locked door.

Andy wouldn't have minded her hurry so much, but he knew the tall man standing in front of the door was the lure.

Chapter Eight

Caro flew to her door, fumbling in her pocket for the key. "Hi. I've been out detecting."

"Isn't your friend coming in?" The lock stuck, and Linc reached for the key. He turned and waved, but Andy was already down the street.

Caro felt a sudden twinge of guilt. She should have asked him in for a coffee.

"What did you mean you were out detecting? Are you a detective, too?"

She shoved open the door. "Come on in. I shouldn't have taken off, but I've been helping Andy try to find who stole his paintings."

"He paints?"

"You probably haven't heard of the Carrington pictures?"

"Your friend is that Carrington? Really? I'm not knowledgeable about art, but even I have heard about the Carrington paintings."

"He's gaining attention. Want some coffee? Tea?"

"Tea sounds good."

"Go ahead and look around. I'll be back in a jiff." Caro hurried to the mini kitchen and ten minutes later, she carried the two mugs back into the shop where Linc sat at the counter. "I'm not much of a tea drinker, but when I do, I have to have the best. Tea Snob, my brother calls me."

"Never could stand tea as a kid." He held up her notepad. "Not bad."

"Just a few preliminary thoughts on a possible play for your church." Caro sat on one of the stools, whirled it in a circle, then sipped at her tea.

"What's the price?" Linc pointed at the ballerina music box. "My mother collects music boxes, and I'm always on the lookout for ones she doesn't have."

Caro walked over to it, twisted the tiny key, and listened to the tinkling music pour out of the box. For a second, she forgot where she was. "Sorry. It's not for sale."

"You attached to it?" Linc's dark eyes twinkled at her.

"Not really." She watched the tiny ballerina twirl around and around. "It's kind of the store mascot, I guess."

More like the symbol of my life. It wasn't that she was so fond of it. At all. In fact, most times it irritated her. The constant reminder urged her, in a mechanical way, to do something with her life.

The lonely ache in her heart felt like the brooding before a storm. Her gaze flicked to Andy's storm painting. She shrugged again, as if to shed the weight. "I'll sell you about anything else. We've got a few other music boxes here and there."

Linc chose an antique-looking church house that played "Amazing Grace." When he'd paid for it, he sat down beside her and laid out what Community Church wanted. Caro listened, nodded, asked questions, and noted the tangled way his dark hair lay against his head. She swallowed. “Are you married, Linc?”

Er-r-g-gh. Had she really asked that? But Toby and Andy had said Linc could be married. She’d put the question to rest right now.

“No, I’m not. My wife died two years ago.”

“I’m sorry.” Yet she couldn’t stop the little jolt of pleasure his confession had given her.

“We were childhood sweethearts, and she was the love of my life.”

Uh, oh. A definitive look of loss played across his face, and Caro knew he’d been very much in love with his wife. And maybe still was.

Much quieter, she asked, “Do you have children?”

The corners of his eyes crinkled. “Two. A boy and girl. Dwight Lincoln, Jr. and Ashley Dawn. Seventh and ninth graders.”

“You must be crazy about them.”

“I adore them.”

For a moment, the expressions flit across his face like a moving screen. Then he turned back to her and an impish grin widened his lips. “In case you were going to ask, I do date, but have no steady relationship.”

Interesting. Her spirits perked up.

He gave her a sideways glance. “I thought about asking you if you’d like to have supper this evening.”

How could this happen? Caro wanted to pull her hair, but instead glowered, and Linc laughed. “Is it that distressing of an offer?”

“I can’t. I have a youth group tonight, and I don't have a speaker yet.” She wailed her answer then snapped her fingers. “Hey. Why don't you speak to them? We usually have a lively discussion, then move on to other activities."

If only she'd done her usual Monday night preparation for the youth gathering, she wouldn't be asking an almost-stranger to fill in. But what he didn't know...

"I'm no speaker. They won't want to hear me." He shook his head and held up both hands.

"It's only for a half hour or so. Come on. They love new speakers."

"I don't know. You've never heard me. Thank God."

"That's no problem. A simple talk would suffice. Nothing elaborate. So you'll do it?" She let her voice plead with him.

"Well, you may wish you hadn't asked, but I can try."

"Great. The kids will love you."

"I doubt it." A wry expression crossed his face as he stood. "Do you oversee this group yourself?"

"No way. I have two excellent helpers. You've met Andy. The kids adore him. And there's Ryle Sadler who moved here a couple years ago. Both of them keep everything on an even keel, make sure the teens don't get too rambunctious, and supervise our outings, too."

"Sounds like a great operation. I'd better get going. When do you think you can have a rough copy of our play ready?"

"Two months?"

"Perfect."

They shook hands, and by the time he'd left, she'd turned back into the store to wait on several customers.

At noon she hurried to put the "closed" sign in the window and locked the front door. She stretched, then took the stairs two at a time.

"Hey, there, Angel girl. Keeping the mice at bay?" Caro strode to the kitchen and jerked open the fridge door. Grabbing a cola, she frowned at the empty box. When her diligent search turned up nothing but the same contents she, Toby, and Andy had had a few days ago and a few cans of soup, she opted for the cream of tomato, opened, and heated it. Settling at the table to enjoy her lunch, she spread the newspaper and read over the first page.

After scraping her bowl clean, she turned the pages and scanned the advertisement section, looking for the new one Toby had just submitted for Undiscovered Treasures.

She read it, pleased at the wording. Toby did such a good job writing an interesting ad every month or so. Then her gaze traveled down the columns, seeking her own simple advertisement for her plays. A tingle of pleasure spread through her as she stared at it.

The thought of Lincoln's request for their special play gave her a joy she seldom felt. But more than that was the results that could come from the purpose of the play.

She flapped the page, adjusting it for better readability, and let her gaze scan down through the other ads. Her gaze riveted to a stop at the sight of one. *Females needed to sit for an artist. Few hours a week. Please respond by calling: 555-3401.*

Caro stared at the number. Was that...her Andy's? She squinted and held the paper close to her face as if she couldn't see it. 555-3401. It *was* Andy's office phone number. She read the ad again, then sat back in her seat.

Andy was advertising for girls to sit as subjects for his artwork? Since when did he do portraits on a daily work basis?

Why hadn't he asked her? On second thought, how did he have time to do portraits when he had the contract with Regency's to fulfill?

Best thing to do was call and ask what he was doing.

No, she couldn't do that. Andy didn't have to answer to her. It was none of her business anyway what he did. For that matter, why did she care?

But she did. The thought of Andy spending hours every day in the presence of gorgeous girls sent her heart into a tailspin. Was she worried about him? Worried the quiet man who'd been in her life, all her life, would be taken in by a beautiful face and hard heart?

When she strode into her bedroom and stared in the mirror at herself, the image reflecting back at her was anything but enticing. A straggly bit of hair had fallen from the clip she'd used to pull it back this morning. She lifted it and studied the dull strand. Why didn't she have the beautiful white blond color of Starli's hair? Or even a honey blond would do. Instead she was saddled with this...mouse color.

She frowned at herself, and that brought her attention to her wide mouth. Yikes. Decent lips but much too wide.

Abruptly she turned away, decision gripping her. Couldn't she change? With help? Starli was gone, and she wouldn't ask her anyway. Starli's look of queenly elegance wasn't for her. But Toni could help her. Toni loved simplicity.

Then she remembered baby Dani's teething problems. Would she have time for her now with that going on and her construction business?

Maybe Toby could suggest someone? She cringed at the thought of his teasing. No, she couldn't ask him.

Knowing everyone in Appleton didn't help if she wasn't comfortable enough to ask such a personal favor.

Toby might know what was going on with this ad of Andy's. She picked up the phone and started to tap his number, then hit the off button. Why not call Andy and ask about the ad as if she was a girl interested? See what Andy said?

She could find out what she wanted and have some fun doing it. She lifted the receiver again and punched in Andy's number. When he answered, she softened her West Virginia twang. "Hello. I was calling about the ad in the Charleston Post."

His quiet voice came through the phone. "Yes. I'm looking for girls who would be willing to sit for a variety of scenes I need. There will be different settings but we can discuss that later."

What did that mean? Where else could you do portraits but in a studio or maybe outside?

"Could I meet you? Shouldn't we talk? I'm

definitely interested." Caro urged the man on the other end.

Andy hesitated. "I'll let you talk to my secretary. She can set up a time for us to meet."

When Stephanie spoke into the phone, Caro asked, "Exactly what would I have to do?"

The assistant's voice was a tad bit sarcastic. "Pose. Mr. Carrington needs photogenic girls for a new project with specific requirements."

Minutes later, Caro set the phone receiver down in slow motion. So it was Andy. The assistant's description had been vague, yet Caro was concerned. What was their friend getting himself into? More than he realized?

~*~

After she closed the store that night, always early on Fridays, Caro spent an hour planning the evening activities for the twenty-some young people who would be at the church. She loved working with them. They kept her on her toes. She was proud that nothing they'd proposed—and so far it hadn't been too far out—had been activities she couldn't keep up with. Whether it was the wild rapids rafting that had ended up being a weekend excursion or the roller blading challenges some of them loved, she'd had fun participating as much as they had. Not as good as them, but she'd tried it all.

When the phone rang at five thirty, she snatched up the receiver.

"Want me to stop by and pick you up tonight?"

Andy. She couldn't remember the last time she'd ridden with him to youth meetings.

"Linc's going to speak tonight to the kids."

There was a long pause. "I guess you both could squeeze in the bug."

Why would he automatically think she and Linc were riding together? Still, maybe she'd have a chance to find out what Andy was doing. "Come on by, and we'll see what happens."

Thirty minutes later, she opened the door to find both Linc and Andy standing there. Double wow. "Come on in. I've just got to grab a couple things."

"She means..." Andy looked at the taller man. "...she's got to make a couple more phone calls, collect her stuff for tonight, and comb her hair."

"Smartie." Caro wrinkled her nose at him. "I am ready. I've got to grab some papers. Be right back." Her voice trailed behind her as she flew up the stairs.

When she returned she handed a box to Linc, a stack of pamphlets to Andy, and picked up her own satchel. "I'm ready."

Linc insisted on driving. At the car, Caro was torn between sitting up front with him, or sitting in the back so she could stare at Andy and try to figure out what he was up to. In the end she slid into the back seat.

As the two men chatted on the ten-minute ride, Caro kept quiet and listened. Though Linc asked questions about Andy's art, none of it brought her any closer to finding out what was going on with her brother's best friend. That is, until she prepared to gather her rather messy satchel, and papers floated to the floor. Annoyed, she bent to retrieve them. Her gaze caught the scribbled-upon paper lying on the floor. It'd been crushed—loosely, but the page was still readable, and she gave it a quick glance.

It was a list of names. Artists? Could be, but right now, it meant nothing to her. Except Linc had insisted he had little knowledge of the art world, so why would a *list* of artists be in his vehicle? If it was such a list. Hmmm.

Debating, Caro's hand hovered over it. It'd obviously been discarded, so wouldn't that mean it was up for grabs? She'd like a closer look at the list. Some of those names looked familiar but she wouldn't know until she studied it more fully.

She'd talked herself into it and grabbed at it as Lincoln opened her door. Discreetly, she shoved it to the bottom of her jacket pocket.

No time for studying it now.

At the church the young people demanded all her attention, with none to study about the paper, Linc or Andy. The Youth Praise Band led the others in several rousing worship songs while Caro, Andy and Ryle Sadler monitored the group. She listened as Andy confidently prayed for the young people, and with his help, Ryle passed out the pamphlets informing the kids of the next excursion the church planned for them.

During activities, she caught sight of Andy with a redheaded young woman. Caro stopped her work and eyed the two. It looked as if they were the best of friends. Once Andy threw back his head with a real belly chuckle, and she sniffed. Cute red heads must be right up Andy's alley.

After introducing Linc to the teens, she settled in a back seat, and when Andy strode to the back too, scooted over so he could sit beside her. Instead he took the seat between Ryle and Cute Red Head.

Caro plunked her notepad on the empty seat and tried to block thoughts of Andy Carrington from her mind.

She tried. She really did. But half way through Linc's thirty-minute talk, she found her mind wandering to Andy's enthusiastic speech from last week. He'd woven in some history to make his point about overcoming temptations and had accented his words with vivid drawings that had kept the young people on the edge of their seats.

She stared at the tall, dark man up front. He was so good-looking. Stunning. Just the sort of man she'd dreamed of. And his car—well, it was something to swoon over.

Caro squinted at Linc standing in front of the room. She hadn't much cared for the tone in his voice when he talked about his deceased wife. Like he hadn't quite gotten over her. Did he compare every other woman to her? It didn't bode well for the future of a new Mrs. Tillis.

She looked around the room to see how the kids were responding to Linc's talk and frowned when she saw two of the boys engrossed in some kind of hand-held electronic game. Across the room, two girls were whispering, and several were slouching in their seats, tapping their fingers and glancing around. What was wrong?

She zeroed her attention on Linc again. What was he saying?

Something about...about...She glanced at Andy. There was the tiniest frown on his forehead, and his lips set in a straight line. What was he thinking?

And what was Linc talking about? Something about history? Ancestry? The importance of being true to your parents? Probably important, but he wasn't holding the kids' attention.

Caro's heart sank as the realization sank in. His subject might be okay, but his voice was so toneless, so boring, it wasn't getting across.

The handsome man up front suddenly laughed and held up both hands. "Time to stop. Let me turn this back over to your leader. Caro?"

As Caro called on one of the more mature teens to pray a dismissal prayer, her gaze met Andy's over the bowed heads. A shared look. She'd made a mistake today. Linc might be the prince she'd dreamed for, but he most certainly wasn't a speaker.

Chapter Nine

Caro hurried to collect the material she needed to take home, well aware Linc stood near the door, waiting. Her gaze caught sight of Ryle and Cute Red Head walking toward Andy.

Stuffing the papers she held in her satchel, she called out as she strode toward the back of the room. "Andy. Wait. Are you riding with us?"

His brown eyes were soft as he swiveled to look at her. "Sorry. No, Ryle and Lauren are giving me a ride home. Thanks, anyhow."

As if he'd tossed a baseball at her head that effectively stopped her in her tracks, Caro halted her advance toward him and stared. Andy had already turned back and his face lit up when the new girl murmured to him.

Were they talking about her? Maybe because of all the times she'd laughed at him she was getting pay back? She shook her head. No, Andy wouldn't laugh at her. Why should she be paranoid?

Andy held out an arm, and Cute Redhead looped hers through his and Ryle's. Laughing, the trio exited the room without a backward glance.

The instant the recreational room emptied, Caro felt the loneliness spread through her body like a damp mist settling over a West Virginia valley.

Linc moved toward her, his dark features drawn and the tiniest bit ashamed, and Caro shook herself out of her mood. Here she had a stunning man to take her home. Was she going to moon over *Andy*?

No, she wasn't. She'd dreamed of this happening, wished for it and prayed for it.

"Let me carry that for you." He reached for her satchel, and she let him take it.

As they walked out to his oversized SUV, he shoved back his sleeve to check the time from the gold watch on his wrist. "It's nine. We have time for a snack. Interested?"

"Let's go to the Coffee House for dessert."

"Sounds good."

Linc's strong voice rumbled on in the darkness of the SUV as they drove to the coffee shop, but Caro's mind wandered. She wondered if Andy had gone straight home and if the Cute Red Head had her sights set on Andy.

She remembered Andy's short, but emphatic talks on the off nights he spoke at the youth meetings, and how confident he was when he stood in front of the young people. He bonded with them easily. They admired his art, enjoyed and participated in the topics he brought to their attention, but most of all, they returned the love they felt from him.

He was an excellent youth assistant.

As they walked into The Coffee Shop, a jolt of pleasure shot through her when Linc clasped her hand. She corner-eyed him to check on his expression. Well, if he didn't look love-struck, at least he didn't look bored.

She saw them as soon as they entered the

shop. Sitting at a table, Ryle, Andy, and Cute Red Head sat sipping lattes. For a second, she stood stock-still, her earlier joy short-lived.

Then Andy looked up and saw her. His laughing eyes sobered, and almost immediately he stood and beckoned.

Caro tugged on Linc's hand and led him across the room with her. She watched as Andy took charge, pulling another table to join theirs. He scooted chairs, and without realizing how he did it, when they were seated, Caro sat on one side of him. Linc had taken a seat on the far side of the red head.

How had that happened? She glanced at Andy. He gave her a roguish grin and turned away to answer a question tossed at him from one of the others.

Red Head's voice broke into her thoughts. "Andy, aren't you going to introduce me?"

"Of course. Sorry, Lauren. Caroline, let me introduce Lauren Stephens from New York. Her father owns a large art company. Lauren, one of my best friends, Caroline Gibson. The gent on your left is Lincoln Tillis from Clarksburg. And you already know Ryle."

"Hey." Lauren arched her neck and peered coquettishly at Linc. "What's a handsome guy like you doing in West Virginia?"

Amidst the teasing rebuttals to her slurring comment, Caro bit her lip to keep back a sarcastic remark in defense of her beloved state.

Lauren turned from Linc's attention and said something to Andy who laughed and patted the redhead's hand.

She'd never seen Andy so friendly with any

female.

Except her.

The words mocked her as she remembered his teasing, the tugs on her braids as children, the awkward pats on her back when Toby had carried his taunts too far, and she'd cried. Andy's shy notes of affection and attempts to hold her hand as a teenager had changed eventually into a more serious adult whose gaze followed and worshipped her from afar.

Jealous. The spontaneous inward accusation stabbed at her, but she tossed it aside. Nonsense. Not when handsome Linc Tillis eyed her with those clear eyes of his.

Andy was an innocent though. A basic country guy, how would he know when a new girl was playing with his affections? *Was* he being duped by a pretty face? If so, it was her duty to keep that from happening. After all, Andy was Toby's best friend. She needed to save him.

From what? The words flapped in her mind like a flag, but she slammed the door on that. No one had ever mistaken her for a coward.

When Lauren leaned toward Andy again, and cooed at him, Caro didn't hesitate to move closer so she could hear.

"I'd really like to see the high school drama club's musical, Andy. This is the last weekend they're performing. Are you free tomorrow?"

Lauren's cheeks were rosy, and she looked absolutely adorable. Even Caro had to admit it, and if the girl hadn't set her sights on Andy, she thought she might even like her.

"He's already seen it." Caro tried to take the edge from her voice.

"Oh."

"We went the other night. It was very good, but then the kids always do well, don't you think?"

"I...I wouldn't know. Well, let me take you to lunch tomorrow, Andy? We have a lot to talk about." Lauren's cheeks creased in dimples.

Caro bit down hard on her tongue. She would kill for dimples like that. Why did she have to get the big mouth? "Oh, dear. Weren't we going to do some more investigating tomorrow, Andy? I figured I'd close the shop about eleven and take a long lunch."

For a moment, Andy looked at Caro, and she wanted to squirm. He knew she'd been haphazard with interest on when to investigate again. He had a right to wonder what on earth was going on. She let out a breath when he answered.

"That's right, we are. Lauren, we do need to talk. What about breakfast?"

"Why don't we all go to the musical at Charleston? If I remember right, they're putting on "A Midsummer Night's Dream" next month. I could check on it and reserve seats for everyone." Linc's gaze flew straight to Caro.

Lauren squealed and turned to Andy. "Sounds like fun. Let's. What night?"

"Friday's the best, I think." Caro spoke up. "How shall we pair up? Andy..."

"Friday it is." Linc drew her attention back to him by giving her a roguish wink. "Caro will go as my date. The rest of you can work out your own dates."

Everyone laughed, and Caro watched as Lauren clasped Andy's arm and grinned up at him, those dimples flashing.

Possessive, wasn't she?

The best looking guy in the room seemed to like her, and she liked him. There wasn't a thing she could do to save Andy now, tonight. She might as well make the best of a date with the man she'd always dreamed about.

Minutes later, as everyone stood to leave, Andy whispered to her. "What is going on with you? You were almost rude to Lauren, and I don't like it. She's important to me."

With a sinking heart and a glance at Lauren to make sure the woman wasn't listening, Caro whispered back. "I thought she was being too pushy. She has no plans to live in West Virginia, Andy."

"What has that to do with me?"

His voice was the sternest she'd ever heard it.

"Well, you know," The heat in her cheeks burned worse than any sunburn she'd ever experienced. "If you think—I mean, if you two—"

"You mean if we fall in love?" Andy turned and stared at Lauren standing at the door with Linc and Ryle, her hair a bright red flame. "She likes my home. What makes you think she wouldn't want to live here—at least part of a year?"

"You just met her. What are you thinking?"

"I'm not thinking anything, Caroline." Andy swiveled back to her. "You started this conversation."

Caro wanted to stomp her foot. She refused to back down. "You're in over your head with her."

"I think I can take care of myself."

With a last glance, he headed back to his new friend, and Caro wanted to do her own clutching. When Andy took Lauren's arm and walked away, the desolation inside her filled her eyes with tears. So much for appreciation of all her worry over him. If he got in trouble, then it was on him. She'd tried.

The drive home was quiet and seemed overly long. Linc's sudden comment had her bumping her elbow when she jumped.

"Sorry about bombing the speech tonight. I told you I'm no speaker."

She could see his mouth crook up in a smile that would make any female swoon. Her soft heart went out to him. She'd gotten him into that. It wasn't his fault.

"Don't worry about it. I coerced you into it. I should have listened to expert advice since you know yourself better than I do. Anyhow, the kids will have forgotten about it by the time Andy talks with them next week."

"That guy ranks pretty high with you. Are you interested in him?"

"Andy? He's my brother's best friend. Why do you say that?"

A shrug. "I just thought you were a little protective tonight. I don't want to interfere in a serious relationship between you two."

Caro opened her mouth to refute the comment, choked, and coughed. When she could speak, she gasped, "No. Nothing like that. I've known Andy all my life. I guess he's my friend, but nothing more."

"Good." He reached for her hand. "You're refreshingly different from most girls I've known. I think I'd like to get to know you better."

Her heart stopped. She knew it. She patted her chest just in case. She didn't want to pass away right now after receiving such an offer. *Give me just a little more time, God.*

"Me, too."

"You, too? You want to get to know yourself a little better?"

He was teasing, and Caro loved it. She was so used to Toby harassing her, she must be missing it. "I meant, I'd like to..."

If his comment hadn't lifted her spirits, his laughter would have. "I know what you meant. I was teasing you."

He pulled in front of Undiscovered Treasures and swung open the door. The stroll to the door went way too fast. When they stood in front of her door, he said. "Shall we plan on a dinner soon?"

"I'd like that, Linc."

~*~

Andy dropped Lauren off at her hotel, in spite of her plea for a nightcap, and stood at the curb, waiting on the signal to change. There wasn't much traffic, not at this time of the night in Appleton, but he liked the lingering and quiet. Gave him time to reflect on how his life was going and on the girl he loved who seemed determined to shun him for life.

The light changed, and he stepped into the street to cross. The sound of a powerful car engine revved somewhere close by, but he paid no attention. He'd be across and at his car in a second—

Out of the dark, a big car—looked like an

old gangster type of car—turned the corner and was on him. No head lights illumined his figure, and for a long second, he froze. Surely it saw him. He had the right of way.

He could hear it shifting, and if anything it sped up and seemed to adjust its aim—right at him. He held up one hand, and then realizing it wouldn't stop—by accident or on purpose, he jumped. And felt the heavy fender give him the bump that sent him, thankfully, fully out of the way.

Andy rolled in the street until he was against the curb, and then he lifted his head and stared after the car. It didn't stop, only screeched around the next corner, the sound of its engine fading as the seconds passed.

He eased himself up, gently feeling the bruise on his hip and the scrapes on his face and arms. At least he wasn't lying in the gutter—dead.

There wasn't any way he could chalk this up as an accident. Not with all that was happening with his work right now.

Whatever was going on, someone was playing a very dangerous game, and it looked like he was the intended victim.

~*~

Caro lingered at the upstairs apartment front window and stared down on the dark street below. She should be rapturously happy. A real date with Lincoln Tillis. A sigh escaped her lips.

The paper she'd lifted from Linc's SUV didn't bode well for their relationship. The list of artists—if that's what it was—and the scribbled notes about each one was a question she needed answered. Why would he have a list like that? He'd given no indication he was interested in artists or paintings or anything else to do with them. Was he a shy artist hiding his talent from others? That still didn't explain why he needed a list of five other artists with information about each one.

Did it?

She should put Andy out of her mind and quit worrying about him. He hadn't declared interest in Lauren Stephens tonight, but the way his eyes had lit up when the girl had spoken to him told her there was a spark between them just waiting to be fanned into a raging inferno of love. Her carefree laugh and the casual way he'd guided her out of the restaurant had spoken volumes.

Stop it. She bit her lip. Since when had she become Andy's keeper? She never had been, and she wouldn't start now. He could take care of himself, he'd said. Well, let him.

Caro slapped her hands together as if dusting them. No more worrying about him. She had too much to do. Wooing Linc, for one thing.

She closed her eyes and leaned her head against the glass of the window then opened them when a car zoomed by. Andy's sky blue car? What would he be doing on her street? He should be home working on another ghastly painting.

Her imagination was running rampant. Sky blue cars and Lauren's interest in Andy, no doubt.

Scooping up Angel, she laid her cheek against the cat's soft hair. "I wonder if Andy is really planning on investigating tomorrow, or did he agree with me to help me save face?"

The thought wasn't all that pleasant. Why shouldn't Andy have a friend—a special friend? She didn't want him.

Then what was this nagging sensation of losing something valuable, creeping over her? Why was she so depressed in spite of the date ahead with Linc? She did want to go with Linc, didn't she?

Caro stroked the cat in her arms. Of course, she did. It's what she'd wanted with all her heart. A big, gorgeous hunk of a guy riding into her life in a white luxurious car. Or in this case, a dark SUV, which was just as good.

She was done worrying about Andy. No more thoughts of him. None.

Caro prepared for bed and snuggled under the cool sheet. She felt Angel curl up at her feet and yawned, the contentment warming her body. A date with Linc in two weeks.

No more thoughts of Andy. No more thoughts of...Andy.

Chapter Ten

For the next few days, the phone rang off its hook.

Stephanie peered over at him when there was a break. “That’s it. I’m turning away any more who call.”

“Do that.” Andy nodded and groaned. “Fourteen interviews. It’ll probably take three or four days.”

His assistant glanced at the calendar she used to keep track of Andy’s business appointments. “Two days. Back to back, I grant you. But it’ll be over that much sooner. I figured you’d like that better.”

“I don’t like any of it.” He glanced at her. “When did you schedule the interviews?”

“Next week. Monday and Tuesday.” Her voice was brisk and all business. “In fact, they might prove quite interesting. Some of these girls had, uh, some good references.”

His grunt was anything but pleasant. “I’d rather spend my time painting. I don’t have time for this. Sure you won’t...?”

“Nope. I won’t know what kind of looks to choose for what you want. Sorry, you’ll have to do this.”

“Why did I know you would say that?”

~*~

Andy was hungry for something sweet. He slipped down the hall to the kitchen, raided his pantry, and sliced a huge chunk of the chocolate cake Lauren had brought over. With one finger he swiped up the crumbs. Delicious. Wherever she'd bought it—he wanted the name of the bakery.

In a distant part of the house he heard the phone ring and wondered if yet another girl had called about the ad he'd placed in the paper. Shrugging, he headed back to his studio.

Stephanie's low voice caught his attention as he passed the office. Either she didn't realize the door was cracked just enough to allow her words to carry or she didn't care.

"He's gone to get something to eat."

A pause.

"He suspects nothing." Another brief silence, and her voice lowered. "Uncle B...knows..., but—"

Was Stephanie talking about him? His heart sank.

"A scare probably. Nothing more. Next time—"

Andy moved on down to his studio and stood at the doorway thinking.

~*~

"Your next appointment, Andy. Carol Gibb."

Andy continued to scribble his thoughts about the last girl he'd interviewed, but motioned with one hand to the newcomer, not bothering to look up. "Please have a seat. I'll be with you in a sec."

From the edge of his mind, he listened to the rustle as she moved to the sofa and sat. In seconds, a tapping rhythm caught his attention, and he looked up.

Caroline Gibson sat on the sofa, her fingers tapping out an impatient beat. “Are you going to keep me waiting forever? Did you make the others wait?”

“Caroline?”

“Caro. I’m your next interviewee.”

“You’re Carol *Gibb*?”

An impish twinkle sparkled from her hazel eyes. “My alias when I’m working undercover.”

Andy couldn’t hold back the grin matching hers. “I should have guessed but didn’t see any of the names before today. Why are you working undercover? Are you following up clues on my missing paintings?”

“No. I’m following up my curiosity on why you’re trying to hire girls from everywhere to sit for your paintings. In other words, I’m being nosy.”

It was such a pleasant sensation to see Caro exhibit interest in him he wanted to give out a shout and hug her. He glanced at her still mutinous expression. Hmmm. Maybe he should just thank God for this unexpected blessing.

“I’m working on samples to include in a resume I’m sending out shortly.”

“And you need a million prett—girls?”

Had she been about to say pretty? She *was* jealous. Good.

“Not a million. Just fourteen, counting you.”

She stood and walked over to a window. “Why didn’t you ask me? Or Toni? Or some of the girls from church?”

He wasn’t about to tell her his concentration would be shot if she sat across from him. He’d get nothing done. And he sure wasn't about to tell her it wasn't exactly the type of painting he usually did.

"I needed girls I don't know, Caroline. People whose personalities I don't know. People to pose so I can concentrate on my painting and not on questions they might shoot my way. I didn't want to stop and think up answers to comments from Appleton's citizens. I didn't want to think about them. Just my work."

"That makes a difference when you paint?"

"Absolutely."

Stephanie stepped into the room. "Are you about ready for your next interviewee?"

When Andy nodded, Stephanie ushered in a tall, willowy blond. "Your next interviewee, Andy. Rikki Renae."

"I'll be just a minute, Rikki. Make yourself comfortable." Andy took Caro's arm and led her across the room. "I've got to go now."

"I still can't understand why you have to have a gazillion girls prancing around in here." Caro shot a scowl at the girl lounging on the sofa she'd vacated minutes ago. She lowered her voice. "She's not very pretty. Not like Toni or Starli."

Andy looked over at the girl. "They don't have to be pretty, just interesting."

"I still..." Caro started to speak, then clamped her lips together. "Never mind. It's really none of my business. Why am I making such a huge fuss? And wasting your time on top of it?

"I never consider talking to you a waste of time. Want to sit in while I interview...what's her name? Of course, you'll have to be quiet. I'll do the talking."

"Are you serious?"

"Sure, come on."

"Wait. What happened to your forehead?"

"This?" He touched his head and lowered his voice. "Would you believe a car nearly ran me down Friday night?"

"Andy, no." She wanted to smother him in a hug, but decided that wasn't the right action considering her designs on Linc. "Do you know who—?"

"Have no clue. Now, I have to talk with this girl. If you're sitting in..." He ushered her to his desk, motioned for her to take another seat, then settled behind his monstrous desk.

"I'm Andy Carrington. So you're interested..."

He was done in fifteen minutes. The girl, though tall and thin, was sulky and uncooperative with her own ideas of what she wanted to do.

Andy was much more interested in watching the expressions flit across Caroline's interesting face. If he weren't in love with her, he'd take her for a model any day.

He could see her in a prairie outfit of the 1800's, the wind blowing through her hair, one hand raised to shield her face as she stared into the distance. That thoughtful expression in her eyes would make any onlooker wonder if perhaps she was looking for her man to come home.

Or maybe he could paint her in a beach scene, her eyes dreamy, her wrap around cover billowing around her, her skin flushed from the sunrays. Then...

Andy jerked himself out of his musings to

find Caroline's gaze on him.

"What were you thinking about? Rikki Renae? You had the dreamiest look on your face."

"You."

"Me?"

"You. I was thinking of painting you."

"Why would you do that?"

Andy let his eyes answer her question.

In a flash, Caro was on her feet. "I've got to go. Thanks for answering my questions."

The woman he loved was running away again while he sat at his desk unable to stop her. He pursed his lips in a soundless whistle and fingered the notebook holding the sketches he'd done of Caroline, just waiting till he could do them in paint. His gaze traveled to the far end of the room where, covered by a cloth, stood an easel with the nearly-completed, replacement painting he'd done. Someday he hoped to hang it in his—their home.

She's an owl sickened by a few days of my sunshine. You can't run away from my love, Caroline.

Chapter Eleven

Caro set the ladder against the wall of shelves that was home to the assortment of antique jars, vases, and bowls Toby constantly brought home. She stood back and eyed the shelves. She'd been meaning to get these cleaned for ages and had kept putting off the job. Dusting was not her favorite thing to do.

She collected dusting rags and polish, then selected a CD to listen to while she worked. She had at least four hours before lunch, and she planned to have this whole wall done before then.

Twisting the knob on the stereo, she sang under her breath with Michael Buble as he sang his latest hit.

The thing was, she couldn't get Andy's words from yesterday out of her mind. Thinking about her? She wished he wouldn't. It was her fault. She shouldn't have been so...well, the word she'd given Andy was nosy, but she hadn't wanted to tell him she was concerned about him.

That wouldn't be a good thing. Would it?

Three hours later, Caro stood back to survey her work. The wood shelves gleamed from the polish. The room reeked pleasantly of her favorite cleaning smell—lemons—and cleanliness.

Now all that was left to do was to dust the

items that had adorned the shelves and replace them. While she was at it, she might as well rearrange them to make room for the stuff Toby would be bringing home Saturday. Caro dusted several pieces, loaded one arm with two of the jars, and grasped the third with the other as she ascended the ladder. She maneuvered one of them on the shelf, then leaned sideways to shove it farther away.

"What are you doing up there without anyone here to hold this ladder?"

The two remaining jars slipped an inch in her arms when she started, and she tightened her hold on them. Swaying, her right hand clutched at the ladder and missed. She felt her feet slip. For two seconds she teetered. Then with a screech, she let go of the jars and grabbed for the ladder, the shelves...anything to stop her quick slide down the ladder to the floor.

Her feet never touched it.

A strong pair of arms caught her as she fell. As from a distance she heard a grunt. Eyes shut, she let her head fall backward to rest on the very available shoulder and groaned. Her mumble came from lips pressed against the linen material of a collar. "I hope I didn't pull your arms from their sockets."

"I'm used to catching lovely maidens who fall from their castles."

Caro lifted her head and stared into a pair of amused brown eyes.

"Andy?"

"Who else?"

A thousand thoughts swirled through her brain, but she couldn't focus on any one of them.

The amusement left Andy's eyes as he returned her shocked stare for a long moment. Then in slow motion, his face inched closer as he shifted her in his arms. For another second, Andy hesitated, his gaze never leaving her face. When his lips touched hers, Caro closed her eyes again. Her calliopeing thoughts jelled into one. Andy Carrington was kissing her.

Before she could react, Andy pulled away and set her on her feet. With unexpected reluctance, Caro opened her eyes and blinked.

Toby's best friend stood in front of her, smiling as if he'd drunk the best cream in the house.

"Why did you go and do that?"

One side of Andy's lips tipped up. "Your lips invited me."

Her traitorous heart thumped with uncanny agreement. This wouldn't do. She stilled her heart by drawing in a deep breath. "I didn't give you permission to...to..."

Andy's mouth widened into a full-blossomed grin. "Are you trying to say 'kiss you'?"

She scowled at him. When she couldn't hold his gaze any longer, she turned away. "Why are you here?"

"Did you forget we were investigating my missing pictures on your *long* lunch break today?"

The words he'd neglected to say flashed like neon lights in front of her. *You didn't want me to go with Lauren, remember?*

It was time to avoid his gaze. Was that laughter in his voice? She was sure he'd emphasized "long." She infused a touch of dignity in her voice. “Of course, I’ll help you. But I need to finish replacing these pieces first.”

“What do you want me to do?”

Shards from two broken jars littered the floor. She cocked her head and eyed him. “Clean this mess up?”

His answer was an exaggerated bow. “Your wish is my command.”

She opened her mouth to remind him to remember that the next time she refused to go with him somewhere.

“But that doesn't include ridiculous commands from fraidy-cat maidens,” he tossed the remark at her as he left the room.

They set to work and for thirty minutes, Caro listened to Andy’s off-key humming of a specific song-phrase. It sounded suspiciously like one of Toni’s favorite old-fashion tunes. “Gonna live my whole life through...loving you.”

She ignored him and kept at her work. If only he’d stop humming that tune over and over. Caro gritted her teeth and concentrated harder.

At last she set the last antique in place and stepped back to survey her work. “Good job, if I do say so myself. Plenty of space for Toby’s new acquisitions.”

“When will he be home?” Andy dusted off his pants.

“He didn’t say but he always has tons of stuff.”

“Then he should be back in time to join us for the dinner theatre Lincoln's getting tickets for.”

“Probably.” Caro shrugged.

"It's too bad you're not going as my date." Andy glanced at her.

"I don't date my brother's best friends. Period."

"That was definite enough. We'll have to see what we can do about that." Andy poured himself a cup of the coffee Caro had prepared earlier. He sipped at it and made a face. "Go get ready. You've got dust on that freckled nose of yours."

"I don't either." She rubbed at the offending member.

"Do, too." Andy's eyes creased as he teased her, and he reached over to tug at her hair as if she was nine again. "Go."

"Ouch." She slapped at his hand and missed, gave him the best stern glare she could come up with and flew up the stairs straight to the bathroom mirror. She repaired her face, but all the scrubbing in the world didn't rid her nose of the smattering of freckles that adorned it. She sighed and glanced down at her smudged shirt. Might as well change it while she was at it.

What had Andy meant when he'd said he'd have to see about being Toby's best friend? The big question was, what was *she* going to do about *him*?

Why do anything? Why not let nature take its course? Prospects looked great with Linc. Andy would learn soon enough that she wasn't for him. If he hadn't already with Lauren lurking in the background.

Andy's left brow lifted when he saw her. "That color looks good on you."

"This old thing?" Caro glanced down at the

pink T-shirt she'd pulled from her drawer. She hated pink. Was that why she'd picked it? To let Andy know—or herself—that she wasn't trying to impress him?

"You look great in any pastel color. Brings a blush to your cheeks."

"Really? Why haven't you told me this before?" She shrugged into a pink/purple/yellow shirt to top her tee and tied the ends together.

"I tried to, but I think it went in one ear and out the other." Andy grinned. "Besides, Toby has tried to tell you for years, but you just shrug off his expert advice. Which by the way, he learned from me."

"Right. So what colors are good for Toni?" Curiosity raised its ugly head, and she couldn't have stopped the question if she'd tried.

"Bright colors. With her sallow complexion, vivid clothes turn her into a beautiful gypsy. And before you ask, Starli looks great in simple whites and blacks, and certain shades of blues and greens. They're perfect for her coloring with an occasional touch of red. Toni and Starli have been following my advice for years."

"You're kidding. They ask your advice on their clothes?"

"Since we were teens. Someone else could have looked like a regular princess if she hadn't stuck her head in the proverbial sand."

"Meaning me?" Caro tossed her hair back from her face. "I like to be my own person. If people don't like me as I am, then they're not very good friends."

"Well said." Andy applauded. "Not very bright, maybe, but spoken in a true independent spirit that doesn't outwardly care whether she has friends or not."

"Are you making fun of me?" Caro glared at him.

"I wouldn't think of it. I admire you too much. I just wish sometimes..." Andy hesitated.

"You wish what? I am not sweet like Toni, and I definitely have no style or queenly attributes like darling Starli. I'm plain. Plain old me." Yikes. Had her voice wobbled? She could feel her throat tighten. Was she going to cry?

"That's what I like about you. Beneath the devil-may-care attitude, you're all soft and caring. And I know it." Andy reached over and touched her chin, lifting her face toward him. "Don't ever say that again. You're not plain. You just don't make the best use of what you have."

"What do I have?" The words came out whispered and a bit on the fearful side.

The slow gentle smile that curled Andy's lips reached his eyes as he studied her, his fingers still on her chin. "You've got a kissable mouth, expressive eyes, and an adorable nose."

She did? That was the nicest thing she'd ever had said to her. Caro reached up and touched her nose.

"You're a talented playwright and a super youth leader. You run a business that's fun and interesting and fairly successful. How many people have accomplished that in their lifetime?"

"I love doing all those things."

"Exactly. You've got a passionate spirit.

Anything you do is done with a full heart."

"How do you know all that?"

"Wait." Andy held up one hand. "There's more. Best of all, you're loyal to your friends and your values and a spirited Christian. Someday, when you let yourself, you're going to fall hard for the right man."

This was going too far. Since when did Andy Carrington become the expert on her? It was way past time to change the subject. She pulled away from the fingers that lingered on her chin. Tender, burning fingers.

"So. Where do we start our investigating today? If we don't hurry, my extended lunch hour's going to be gone."

A speculative gleam shone from Andy's eyes, but she chose to ignore it. She'd had enough evaluation for today. "What about the red car Jeffrey saw? Isn't there anything we can do about that?"

"What? We haven't got a license plate number, and even if we did, I have no pull with anyone in the BMV."

Defeated before they started. This wouldn't work. "Well, what then? We've got to start with something."

"Why don't we check out the pawn shops?"

"That's a good idea, although I think any thief who would go to the trouble of stealing a painting might be aiming for something higher than that. Why don't we also check out some art galleries? We can start with the area phone book."

They bent over the book. The yellow pages listed one pawn shop in Appleton, one each in two different neighboring towns, and three in

Charleston. There was also a shop that sold paintings, but they were exclusive to the shop's objects. Still, it was someplace else to look.

"I don't think we have time to go to Charleston."

"Not unless you wanted to take the day off." Andy's voice was hopeful. "We could sleuth today and have dinner at a nice restaurant tonight."

That was definite slyness in those brown eyes of his. Thought he was pulling a fast one, did he?

"Can't." She shook her head. "I, Mr. Carrington, have an important date in two days and have work to do. It might be the date of my life."

Now why had she added that tidbit of information? When would she learn to guard her tongue?

"I see."

There wasn't any doubt of it. Andy's eyes radiated messages of definite speculation.

"Besides, don't you remember? I don't date Toby's friends."

"Right. You did mention that."

"I mean, it's much easier if we keep our relationship as friends only."

"Friends is something."

He sounded as if his tongue was in his cheek. What was wrong with Andy? He'd always been so laid back and easy to get along with.

Maybe he was in love with Cute Red Head. Oops. Lauren Stephens. But if he was—why had he kissed *her*?

Chapter Twelve

Caro crossed off the last name of pawnshops from their list. “I guess that does it. None of them have recently bought any paintings.”

Andy set the phone receiver on the counter. “If they’re telling the truth.”

“Why should they lie to us? They don’t know why we’re looking for art work.”

“True enough. What’s next?”

“I’ve been thinking.” Caro flipped her hair from her shoulder.

“Uh oh.”

“Wise guy. We’ve never done anything about your other close neighbors—the Bennett’s. And have you talked with Stephanie?”

“Stephanie. Why?” The strange conversation days ago lit up like a neon sign in his mind.

“Duh. Could be she heisted your paintings? Although I doubt it after her statement of devotion she gave the other day.”

“Could be, but I've always trusted Stephanie to date.”

That sounded like a conditional statement. Was he holding something back? “How long did you say you've known her?”

“Not long. A little over a month, but I'll have to say, so far, she’s been a wonder woman.”

“Does she handle all your business?”

“Of course not. Donald does that. Stephanie keeps me organized at my studio. Orders my supplies. Cleans up after my mess, runs errands, does correspondence, takes calls and handles the customers who show up at my door."

"Little Miss Efficient, isn't she?"

"Stop being catty. That's what she gets paid for."

"Sorry." Would she never learn to keep her opinions to herself? She didn't know Stephanie at all, had only met the girl the one time. In fact, when had she been at Andy's last?

"Let's go to your studio."

"Am I allowed to know what you've got up your sleeve now?"

"I want to talk with this paragon of yours again. Besides, we need to look over the crime scene. Maybe I'll see something you've missed. Fresh eyes and all that."

"Okay if I give Stephanie a call to clear out the mess before we get there?"

Laughing, she stood and waggled her brows at him. "Absolutely not. I want to see it as it is."

Andy groaned. "Why did I think you'd say that?"

~*~

As Andy turned onto his drive, Caro realized anew how beautiful Andy's place was.

"Who would have believed you could have taken your grandfather's rundown home and turned it into this?" Surrounded by woods on three sides, the winding road gave a glimpse of the place from different angles, and every one of them was breathtaking.

"I thank God every day He gave Gramps and me a few years together."

Andy's parents had traveled for business while he grew up, and the care of the boy had fallen to his paternal grandfather. Though his parents had left him their property, once Andy reached twenty-one, he'd promptly sold their place and moved back in with his grandfather.

With the insurance money from his parents' death, Andy had restored the place and set up his painting studio.

But as much as the place tugged at her heart, what caught her attention now was the three vans and the assortment of cars parked in front. About a dozen people were huddled on the front lawn.

"What on earth?" Andy's brow riddled with frown lines.

"Customers?"

"It looks like..."

Caro sat forward and strained to read the sign on the van. Then she saw the antennas on top of the vans. "It's the Charleston television station and looks like two others have joined them. Afraid they'd miss some important news about you, I suppose."

"What on earth?" Andy repeated the words, but Caro didn't think he even realized what he was saying.

He pulled the bug to the side and flung open his door. Caro matched his action and stepped out as he did. The small swarm of people rushed toward them.

"Andrew Carrington?"

"Andy?"

"Mr. Carrington?"

Three mics were thrust in front of him. Andy responded as though each mic was an open-mouthed, venomous snake poised to strike. "What's going on?"

"Will you comment on the thefts of your pictures?"

"Can you describe these works for us?

"Are the police working on this?"

"Who told you they were stolen?"

"Aren't they?" One sleek, dark-haired woman tossed at him, the slyness in her eyes belying the innocent question.

"Y-e-s." Andy swept the group with a glance, caught Caro's attention, and nodded toward the house.

Caro wasn't about to go anywhere. She wanted to know what was going on. Who had told the press someone had stolen his paintings?

The artist held up a hand. "I'll answer your questions, if you answer one of mine."

The group hesitated then a short stocky guy spoke up. "Sure, if we can."

"Who told you I had stolen pictures?"

Stocky guy shrugged. "A tip."

The others nodded.

"Do you mean to tell me some anonymous person tipped three stations about it?"

More nods.

Andy looked flummoxed, and Caro hid a grin. Of all the things she'd seen on Andy's face, she'd never dreamed he'd be stumped.

~*~

Caro left Andy to his popularity with the press. She shoved open the front door and shut it behind her. She wanted to meet Andy's helper, and now seemed as good a time as any without Andy around to stop her questions.

Stephanie stood at the front window watching her boss and the crew of people outside on the lawn. Was that a delighted grin on her face? She glanced at Caro as she entered Andy's studio room and sobered. "I tried to shoo them away. Told them he wasn't home, but they wouldn't listen. Short of calling the cops, I didn't know what to do."

"You could have called his cell phone and warned him."

"He told me not to call him. Said he was going to see his girl. I didn't know if he meant the new girl in town or you. And you're the supposedly Carol Gibb who came for an interview with Andy, aren't you? Why did you come under a false name? I knew who you were the moment I saw you."

Heat rushed to Caro's face. Was his girl Lauren? Or did Andy consider her his girl? The man was enough to drive a sane person insane. "Of course not. I mean, yes, I'm Caro Gibson."

The girl turned away, the odd expression on her face interesting.

Were her comments meant to be snippy? Although stylish, she wasn't a beautiful woman, not even what a person would call pretty, but she carried herself well and looked good.

"What do you think about Andy's missing paintings?"

One shoulder went up, then the other. Stephanie faced the window again and didn't turn around to answer. "Have no idea. It seems kind of funny to me. There wasn't a break-in, at least what Andy and I could tell."

"Maybe the thief knew what he was after. He wouldn't have had to make a mess if he walked in, picked up what he wanted, and walked out again. Does Andy ever leave his doors unlocked?"

"All the time. He had a decent but outdated security system put in years ago, he said, when his grandfather was still alive, but seldom used it. Now he's had a new one installed."

"Did you notice them missing, or Andy?"

"Andy, although about once a week, I go through everything and inventory what he has finished, what he's working on, etc., etc. I usually notice if something's not right, so I don't understand how I missed those two."

"Is there ever a time when no one's here? I mean, what time do you arrive in the mornings? You don't work weekends, do you?

"Why are you so worried about this? Andy reported it to the police." The assistant turned her head to stare at Caro, the least bit of annoyance feathering her words.

Yeah, right. She'd never forget how the police had ignored her friend Starli's complaint that her brother-in-law was harassing her. "Andy is my friend."

"I thought he was your brother Toby's friend, and you—"

Caro ignored the question. "Where were the stolen paintings kept?"

Stephanie swept a hand around. "In here."

"And neither you nor Andy saw anything out of order?"

A well-shaped eyebrow rose.

Wandering around the room, Caro was

careful not to disturb any of Andy's work. The farther she walked and the more pictures she viewed, the more depressed she grew. How could anyone like this stuff?

She dawdled past Stephanie's desk, then paused. "Do you suppose I could have something to drink?"

The tall woman moved away from the window. "I suppose. What would you like?"

"What does he have?"

"Juice, water, tea."

"No soda?"

"In Andy's home? Hardly."

"I'll have water then." Anything to get her out of the room for a few minutes. "With plenty of ice, please."

As soon as the secretary had gone, Caro bent over the desk. What had caught her eye?

A list. A list of—whom? Could it possibly be art dealers? Caro frowned. She wasn't any expert, but she'd never heard of any of these. Why did Stephanie have this list on her desk? Did Andy know about them? Could be there was a very legitimate reason for her to have them.

She cast a glance at the up-to-date computer but hurried footsteps sounded in the hall. Caro's hand hovered over the paper. Should she, or not?

Of course, she should. It was Andy's house, and she *was* investigating for him.

She sauntered over to a large side window and stared out the sheet of plate glass. When Stephanie handed over the glass of water, Caro took it and drank half of it before setting it down on a side table.

The woman had taken a position by the front window again. Caro turned back to the window. What was so fascinating the woman could barely take her eyes off the scene?

But across the spacious lawn, she saw the neighboring house with a man standing at the bordering fence. He seemed to be taking in the action going on in Andy's front yard, given the binoculars he held to his eyes. Was this Andy's neighbor, Mr. Bennett?

Caro checked on Stephanie, who still stared out the front window as if her eyes were glued to the scene, then moved to the French doors, stepped outside and started across the lawn.

The regal-straight, white-haired man stood close to a big oak at what Caro assumed was the property line. She could see his house just behind him, and it wasn't anything to sneeze at. As nice as Andy's home was, this one was twice as prestigious.

She slowed as she neared him.

The man spoke without removing his binoculars. "Have you ever wondered why neighbors seem to have a much more fascinating life than your own?"

"Well, no." Caro blinked. "But I guess I should have. Mine isn't very exciting. In fact, it's quite boring by most standards."

The man removed the binoculars and grinned at her. "Just so. That's the averages. Yet why shouldn't we make our own excitement?" He nodded at the commotion going on at Andy's.

Her mouth dropped open. "You did this?"

"You mean, called the news people?" A shake of the head. "No, I didn't. Although I wish I'd thought of it."

He seemed to be contemplating that thought, his lips spread as if tasting something pleasant.

"But you know who did?"

"Looks like the action's about to wrap up." He nodded toward the news people.

Andy still stood on his front lawn, but the others had begun drifting toward their waiting vehicles.

"I sure would like to know who tipped them about his missing pictures." Caro kept her attention on the man beside her.

"That boy's bound for great things. You rarely find someone who's a decent person along with such talent." He shook his head. "Most artists are so moody, they're fortunate to have a couple good days a month."

"You like his work?"

"Quite taken with it. I've already bought one work I couldn't resist. I predict the prices for them are going to skyrocket in the near future."

Caro glanced at the slim man she'd known forever. He stood with his hands on his hips as if exasperated to the limit.

Her gaze swiveled to Mr. Bennett. Another person who loved Andy's work. Why couldn't she see their value?

"I didn't know you knew Andy that well?"

"Who did you say you were?" The sharp blue eyes studied Caro.

"He's my friend. And my brother's best friend. We've known each other all our lives." She gladly supplied the information. No one could top that qualification, she was positive.

"I see. You'd be the Caroline Gibson who owns the junk shop in town?"

Resentment reared its ugly head. Junk shop? Who did this old bird think he was?

"Excuse me? It's a very profitable antique business."

"Junk too. Yes?" The blue eyes remained fixed on her, and Caro was sure they were laughing.

He thought it was a joke, did he, to get her riled up?

"I'm helping Andy try to find who snitched his paintings." She inserted just a trace of pompousness to her tone. Whoever he was, neighbor, friend, or foe, he needed put in his place.

"I see." He repeated and crossed his arms. "Have you tried talking to his neighbors?"

Duh. "That's what I'm trying to do now."

"So you are." Mr. Bennett chuckled. "But I'm sure there's nothing I can tell you. Right now."

Meaning? The man was superb at avoiding questions.

"You haven't seen anything unusual going on?"

He pointed a finger at her and grinned again. "Little lady, I'm one neighbor who minds his own business. I don't believe in nosiness."

He glanced down at the expensive looking watch on his wrist. "I've got an appointment now. If you'll excuse me? Maybe we can talk again?"

He turned away, but Caro stared after him. He seemed like a harmless old man, but he was sharper than he wanted her to think, and he knew more than he wanted to tell.

He'd said he didn't believe in nosiness. Ri-gh-t. What was he doing with those binoculars glued to his eyes then?

Chapter Thirteen

Andy slammed his car door and started the engine. Shifting the gears, he picked up speed.

"Look at this." Caro smoothed out the list she held.

"What is it?" Andy glanced at the paper.

"It's a list of names. Do you recognize them? Could they be fences for stolen art?"

"I doubt it. Where did you get it?"

"Well, I... Do I have to say?"

"If you want me to answer your questions."

Caro flounced in her seat. "You're worse than Toby. I got it from Stephanie's desk."

"Give it here." Andy held out a hand.

"No way. It's evidence."

"I just want to look at it."

She placed it in his hand and watched as he gave it a couple quick glances. When he looked up, she didn't like the gleam of mirth shadowing his eyes.

"What?"

"It's a list of businesses and people who have ordered at least one of my paintings from Regency's."

"Are you sure?" Caro sighed at Andy's nod. "My big clue just bit the dust."

"I gave it to Stephanie to file." Andy laughed. "You're not quitting, are you?"

"Of course not."

"Are you still pointing a finger Stephanie's

direction?"

Andy wasn't taking her suspicions serious. She ignored his question. "How well do you know your neighbor?"

"Mr. Bennett?" Andy shrugged. "He invites me to one of his dinners two or three times a year. Why?"

"He's a shrewd man. I think he knows something he's not telling."

"What do you mean? You think he knows something about my missing paintings? Do you think he had something to do with them?"

"I don't know. But when I tried to question him, he kept skipping out of answering. He was very evasive."

"Tell me what he said to make you think that."

Caro explained how he'd evaded her questions and his interest in the action on Andy's front lawn with the media.

"Does sound as if he didn't want to give you any answers. Maybe he thought you were too nosy."

"With him holding binoculars to his eyes and spying on his neighbor?" Caro chuckled when Andy cocked an eyebrow at her again as if hearing her say the words had shot a double dosage of doubt into him.

"Let me think about it. Bennett is a very private person. I can't see him butting into my business."

"Well, someone did." Caro pointed out.

"He's got a big dinner coming up. A lot of his former business associates and big shot clients will be there. Want to go as my date?"

"You're invited?"

"Yes. I told you..."

"I know what you said."

"Well, I just so happen to have an invitation to this one, and if you're serious about investigating him more fully...here's your opportunity."

"Why do you like to go? I thought you enjoyed a simple life."

"True. But there're advantages to other lifestyles too. Besides, Bennett is influential, and I'm hoping he'll put in a word or two while I'm there that night. I could use a sale or two."

Andy's sober face caught her attention. He'd only ever worked at part-time jobs, and most of them had been to help out a friend or to encourage someone. His art had always taken front and center with him, and she supposed all their friends had never given a thought otherwise.

Was he hurting for money? "Do you need money? Toby could—"

"No, thanks. I'm good." Andy flicked a glance her way. "So are you going to Bennetts with me?"

"Maybe."

"What does that mean?" Andy zipped around the corner and turned onto her street.

"Maybe I'll go."

"Don't take too long to make up your mind. I'll get someone else to go if you don't want to."

Now, why did he have to go and spoil the day? "Fine. I'll go. It'll give me a chance to check him out."

"Exactly."

"Uh, I was wondering..." Caro swallowed the lump in her throat. This was harder than she supposed.

"What?"

"I thought maybe you could..."

Why on earth had she thought to ask him for help? Surely she could decide what to wear.

Andy pulled to the curb in front of her store. Then he turned sideways. "I won't know whether I can or not unless you tell me. This isn't like you."

Why had she started this? "Can you tell me what I should wear on...on a nice date?"

There. She'd said it. She gave Andy a sideways glance. At least he wasn't laughing. Was he taking her seriously?

"Tell me what choices you have."

Caro sighed. What did she have good enough for a nice dinner?

"Do you have anything black?"

"I think so. But you said I should wear pastels." Caro protested.

"Right. If you have a dressy black bottom, then pick a soft lightweight sweater or fancy blouse. Don't go with white; too harsh for your complexion. Try a pale pink or blue and almost anyone can wear peach."

"I've got a new light rose blouse Toni gave me for my birthday. I haven't worn it. Thought it was too fancy for anywhere I went."

"I remember it. I saw it one day and recommended it to Toni when she wanted something for your birthday. That's perfect. Go with the dark bottom—either black or a dark, dark red, then wear skimpy heels. You do have some, don't you?"

"No..." Caro started to answer him then remembered the heels she and Toni and Starli had each bought together last fall. She'd planned on returning them, then had forgotten to do so until now.

"Yeah, I do. I doubt I can walk in them. I'm used to flats and tennis shoes."

"Get them out and wear them for an hour this afternoon and tomorrow to get used to them. You'll do fine. Just slow down when you walk and try to float."

"Float? Great. It's hard enough to stay on my feet walking, and the man tells me to float. I don't know how to float." Caro leaned her head against the window.

"Come on, I'll show you." Andy swung his door open and motioned.

She joined him on the sidewalk.

"Want to go get your heels?"

"I don't want to learn to float. All I wanted was a hint of what to wear tonight."

"Okay. Okay. Now watch." He gave her an exaggerated example of his interpretation of floating.

Caro giggled when a car drove past, the occupants staring.

"You're going to be the talk of the town."

"What I do for my friends." Andy winked at her.

"You'd do this for Toby?"

"Never. Now, you try it."

Knowing her face was as red as Andy's, Caro strutted down the sidewalk. Andy's instructive voice followed her. "Don't strut. Float. Pretend you're on a cloud."

Caro softened her walk. She hoped the neighbors weren't watching behind their curtains. What a show she and Andy were putting on—and at their age.

"That's better. If you practice your walk every day for a half hour or so, you'll get the hang of it in no time." Andy beamed at her.

Her shoulders relaxed, and she grinned back at him. "I'll never ask you for another thing again, Andy Carrington. It's too embarrassing."

~*~

That evening Andy stared at the envelope. He'd sent his samples in along with his updated resume, and this, he was sure, was the answer.

He noticed his fingers shaking. This could be the deal—the offer—that would change his life. He'd prayed, and now he bowed his head again. *Dear Lord, you know what you want for my life. Help me here—if this isn't what you want—to make the right decision.*

With a sudden move, he ripped open the envelope. Two photos fell out.

Two beautiful young girls posed in skimpy clothing—nothing exactly wrong according to the world's standards, but way worse than he was used to seeing his Appleton friends wear.

He picked up the top one and stared down at it. Lauren Stephens? It couldn't be, yet it was. What on earth was she doing working for this company? Did she realize the requirements could—probably would get worse?

Could he help her? Was it even any of his business?

Slowly he drew out the letter and read.

Mr. Carrington,

We were pleased and excited to receive your resume and the samples you sent. We have reviewed your work; it's very good. In fact, we're extremely impressed, although you would have to bring much more sensationalism into your work to suit our needs.

To aid you in understanding what we're looking for, we have included several different snaps of some of our past successful work. Please look over them carefully.

We have also taken the liberty of setting up a time for you to come to New York to meet with us...

The words of wisdom from King Solomon reverberated through his brain as he sat horrified.

A man shall not be established by wickedness.

Andy read the letter again and frowned. The same word caught his attention. Sensationalism? How far would he be required to go if he signed a contract with this business? Was he prepared to go that distance, even for Caroline?

He dug into his desk for the material he'd first received, flipped through the sheets of paper and pulled out the one with estimated prices on what he could expect if things worked out. He felt a gasp of shock choke from his lungs as the numbers sprang to view. Riches and fame within reach? Did he want them or not?

To do or not to do, that was the question. Paraphrased famous words from Shakespeare. He twisted his lips in a wry grimace. Since when was he tempted to go against his Christian principles?

Since Lincoln Tillis appeared on the scene, a serious contender for Caroline's love. But temptation and yielding were two different things.

He knew what God wanted him to do. The words from Psalmist David, one of his favorite life guiding verses, filled his mind.

Cause me to hear thy loving kindness in the morning; for in thee do I trust: cause me to know the way wherein I should walk; for I lift up my soul unto thee.

If he signed this contract, could he ever lift his soul to God again?

And the answer was no.

Chapter Fourteen

The ringing phone interrupted his depressing thoughts. Andy snatched up the receiver. “Carrington here.”

The booming, overly confident voice of his agent came through the receiver. “Andy, my boy, have I got news for you.”

Andy jerked the receiver away from his ear. “What’s happening, Donald?”

“You heard of The Stephens House of Artwork in New York?”

“Here and there.” What did this have to do with him? They were too big to be interested in someone who was less than already famous even if he had met the big man’s daughter.

“I was at an exclusive party the other night. Stephens was there. Seems he’s branching out into what he calls “discovering modern talent” and launching the artists’ careers.”

“I see. And?”

“He approached me.”

“What are you getting at, Donald?”

“He’s wild to meet you.” The smugness in his agent’s voice was a clue the man was in a good mood. “He attended one of Regency's select auctions—after his daughter called him—and bought the painting—for a heart-stopping price, mind you. He raved about your work. I told him you’d fly to New York tomorrow morning, have lunch, and discuss business. I can't be there till evening, so don't sign anything before I have a chance to go over it. Your flight tickets are waiting at the airport. I'll talk to you late that night or early the next morning."

"But, I have ..."

"I know you have the five-year contract with Regency's. That's minor compared to being connected with Stephens."

"But I'm not sure I can de—"

Too late. The line went dead, cutting off his objection. Typical Donald.

Well, his grandfather always said when one door closes, another opens.

Andy glanced down at the scattered papers on his desk. With recklessness surging through him, he swept the "sensationalism job offer" into his trashcan. So much for that job.

~*~

Thankfully, the late morning air was warm with a light breeze.

The taxi deposited him in front of a posh hotel in downtown New York. Andy stared up at the grand building and felt like a country bumpkin. He glanced down at his clothes. At home, he'd picked out his best chinos and a blue shirt. He'd thought they looked casually business-like in Appleton, but here in New York with all the fashionable people swarming around him, he wasn't so sure.

No time to worry about it now. He was here with only ten minutes to spare.

The doorman was appropriately distant, but didn't cast any scornful glances his way, so Andy figured he couldn't look too much like a pauper.

The elevator operator pushed silent buttons and in seconds, he was thrust onto the sixteenth floor. When the butler opened the door, a second man ushered him toward a door on the left and knocked discreetly. Andy entered the room and caught his first glimpse of Stephen Stephens.

"Carrington." The man who stood with outstretched hand was tall, but not thin. His head of brown hair waved back from a narrow forehead, his eyes were friendly and his manner cordial, in spite of the man's obvious wealth.

After handshakes, Stephens motioned toward a tall-backed leather chair. "Have a seat. Before I forget, rather than lunch, I've reserved seating at a place I think you'll enjoy tonight. All right with you?"

"Of course." Andy settled in the indicated chair and waited on Stephens to begin.

"I've seen your work, Carrington, and I'll have to admit, I'm impressed." Stephens leaned forward. "I don't need to tell you that happens less and less frequently these days."

Andy reminded himself to keep his curiosity and enthusiasm in check. "Thank you, sir."

The man opposite him propped his elbows on his desk and formed his fingers into a teepee. "In fact...I wouldn't hesitate to say you're one of the best I've seen. Ever seen."

Andy inclined his head, but he thought his heart might hammer its way through his chest. "Thank—"

"Don't thank me." Stephens lifted a hand. "You have the talent. You've earned the praise. I haven't done anything—yet, but I want to.

Carrington, I want to sponsor you, make a big name of you. Promote you across the ocean. England. France. Italy. Perhaps even Russia."

He paused and his voice lowered as he allowed his enthusiasm to get the best of him. "Do you realize what I'm saying?"

"Yes, sir, I believe I do. I would be less than honest if I didn't confess I'm interested."

"Ah, I thought you would be. Who could resist?" Stephens sat back with a satisfied smirk.

Andy started to speak, but Stephens talked on.

"I would want your total concentration on our efforts—"

Andy shook his head. "I can't do that. I've already signed a five year contract with Regency's for three paintings a year."

Annoyance flashed across the man's face then was gone. Andy noted how smoothly he moved beyond what couldn't be helped. "Of course, I could get you out of that, if you wanted?"

At Andy's second shake of the head, Stephens nodded. "I thought so. Conscientious guy, aren't you? I like it."

It was time for Andy to state his own conditions. "I'm a Christian, sir. I would have to have the liberty of painting what I'm inspired to paint."

"Nothing too...bold?" Stephens nodded in agreement. "I'm sure we can trust your judgment. I'll have to insist on having the last say on what I promote."

"No problem."

The door to the study opened, and Lauren's

red head peeked in. "Daddy? Coffee? Tea?"

"Come in, Lauren."

In spite of the tray she carried, the girl bounced into the room, her face lit with confidence and happiness. Andy found himself admiring her general enthusiasm.

She set the silver tray on a small table and walked over to him. He stood, and she extended a hand. "It's good to see you again, Andy. I flew here last night when I heard you were going to meet Daddy. He hasn't been able to talk about anything else for days now since he saw some of your work."

"Thank you. I'm glad he liked them. What did you think?"

She cocked her head in a totally unconscious way as she thought about her answer. "I think...your work is pretty profound. Most people would skim right over your hidden meaning, but if you're looking for it, it's very poignant."

This girl was totally likeable, but his heart ached for her too. He wondered if her dad knew what she was into. "Have you had training in art?"

Lauren tilted her head in the direction of her father. "Only what he's taught me since before I could walk. I can remember being perched on his shoulder as he went from work to work. Some of his comments still stick in my mind."

Lauren poured coffee for each of the men, and Andy and Stephens settled down to discuss terms. Lauren, instead of leaving the room, snuggled into a cushioned chair.

When Andy finally stood to leave, she turned to her father. "Daddy, I want to walk Andy down. And in case I don't see you again today, I'm going out tonight to a party."

Stephens lowered his head and looked at her over his glasses. "Not to Ike's Place, I hope?"

The girl rolled her eyes. "I'm not a child."

"No, but you're my daughter and only child. I'll not take any chances with you." Stephens ended the conversation by walking to the huge plate glass window.

A pained expression flicked across Lauren's pretty face, but she said nothing, only took Andy's arm and walked with him to the elevator, her chatter going non-stop. She tilted her head. "I like you, Andy. Can you stay for awhile? You could go with me tonight."

"I think your father vetoed that."

"I love him dearly. He's my favorite father in the world." She wrinkled her nose. "But what he doesn't know won't hurt him."

Andy pulled out the picture from his pocket.

Her gaze rested on his somber face before dropping to the photo. "What is...oh."

When she snatched at it, he pulled it away.

"Lauren, it's none of my business, but what is a beautiful and intelligent girl like you doing in this kind of work?" Andy kept his voice gentle and unaccusing.

"Where did you get this? Whatever you do, don't tell Daddy. He thinks everything I do with my friends is wrong." Lauren shrugged her hair back, her voice raising a notch or two, the tiniest bit of panic in her voice. "I only did it for fun. A bunch of us girls did it for a prank."

A poor one. "I respect you too much to want to see you demean yourself that way."

Lauren tilted her head and gave him a coy look. "But I want you to care about me."

"I'd like you to promise not to do this again. It would mean a lot to me."

"I *want* you to care about me, Andy." She whirled, turning her back to him. "If you won't go to the club, we could go somewhere else. Daddy likes you."

"You're a sweet girl, Lauren, but my heart is already taken. I can't change my feelings."

She tossed him a swift disbelieving look over her shoulder. "It's that Gibson girl in your hick town, isn't it?"

Andy didn't answer.

"You know daddy can really boost your career, don't you?"

"Is that coercion I hear in your voice? Like me, or daddy won't?"

"Maybe." She grinned and whirled to hug him. "No, I wouldn't do that to you."

Gripping his arms, she looked up at him. "I'll think about what you want me to do. I probably won't do the picture-thingy again. Is that good enough?"

"You know it's not." Andy stared down into the girl's blue eyes, distressed at her casual tone. "I'll be praying for you."

As Andy rode the elevator to the ground floor, accompanied by the uniformed operator, he thought about the girl he'd just left. And he thought about the offer he'd received from Stephens.

He stepped outside the building and watched the cars as they streamed by, focused on the rushing sea of humanity as they swept by him, and registered the sounds of the city.

Horns honked, voices blended together, hawkers blared their wares, and sirens screamed in the background. Exciting and vitalizing, but not home.

Andy punched in the phone number of his agent and when Donald answered, he spoke. “I’ve just finished talking with Stephens. He offered me the contract.”

The man’s approval came more as a donkey’s bray than a laugh. “Way to go, Andy. I knew I had a winner when I signed you on. And didn’t I tell you I had my ways of getting you business? More tricks up my sleeve than a magician. You have nothing to fear from here on.”

The man’s enthusiasm was contagious. “Just so long as it’s legal.”

“Stephens has dinner arranged for tonight?”

“Yes.”

“I’ll pick you up at your hotel. How about staying a few days before you head for home?”

“Sure.”

With one hand held up for a taxi, Andy disconnected. If all went as well as his agent thought, he was on his way.

Caroline, here I come.

Chapter Fifteen

The thought struck him as he settled into the back of the cab. He had no clothes with him suitable for a place like Stephens had reserved for tonight. In fact, he had no clothes like that at home either. Had never had a need for them.

He reached forward and tapped the driver on the shoulder. "Know where I can buy a good set of clothes?"

"Sure." The young guy grinned in the mirror at him. "My parents frequent the places even though I wouldn't be caught in a suit. Gimme a few more years, and I might reconsider."

"Just as soon as you land your first big job out of college, huh?"

The taxi driver nodded. "Got that right."

He deposited Andy on a street and pointed out a couple different shops. "Try those. The best and reasonable too."

Andy ambled over to the first one and peered in the window. The image that reflected back his shaggy hair caught his attention. Might as well get a haircut while he was splurging. He opened the door and walked in.

A tall, regal-looking older man approached and spoke in a well-modulated voice. "How may I help you, sir?"

"I need a suit for tonight, shoes, the works."

The man tapped a finger against his lips. "Very good, sir. Follow me, please."

Six hours later, Andy was back in his hotel room, dressed and ready to go. When his agent picked him up that evening in his sport car, they zipped through the city to the restaurant where Donald turned his pride and joy over to the parking attendant. Inside, the maître de' led them to a quiet alcove where Stephens and Lauren sat.

As they approached, Lauren flashed an upward glance at him, her eyes wide with approval.

After greeting them, Andy settled into the chair beside Lauren and studied the radiant girl. Her simple dress belied its expensiveness, yet it suited her and gave her a mature look he liked.

"Why are you staring at me?"

Her whisper barely reached his ears.

"I like the way you look tonight. Simple but beautiful. A perfect young lady."

She dimpled. "Dad insisted I come tonight."

"So you didn't come on your own free will, huh?"

"Well..." She cast a glance at Donald Snelling who'd captured Stephens' attention with a long tale of a proposed project, then corner-eyed Andy. "It didn't take much persuasion. I decided I'd rather see you again then have another night at the same old nightclub."

"You're very flattering."

"But useless?" Her eyes flashed. "Talking about new looks. I didn't realize..."

"What? That I knew how to dress for a place like this?"

"Not quite."

"Of course, you didn't. But it was fun slumming in Appleton, West Virginia with the country boy, wasn't it? You didn't realize how different I could be outside of Appalachia." He let his eyes warm to make sure she knew he was teasing.

"I'll have to admit I've never met someone like you. You don't seem to realize how—uh, important Daddy is. He's very impressed with you."

"He likes my talent."

"That, too." She wrinkled her nose at him.

She was silent for a long while, shoving her meat from one side of the plate to the other, but eating very little. She took a tiny bite, then glanced at him again.

"See what an influence you are on me? I think I need you."

She definitely needed some influence, but he didn't think he was the one for the job.

"There's chemistry between us." She leaned toward him. "We could make a go of it. Give it a try."

"You think that because I'm new to you and different with whom you usually associate with. But I've already told you my heart—"

"I know. I know. The girl in West Virginia." Lauren laid down her fork and folded her napkin. "Are you done eating? Let's take a walk."

Andy glanced down at the half of a rice-stuffed Cornish Hen he'd not yet eaten and wondered what she'd do if he refused. He took one more bite of the Spicy Cranberries heaped in their lemon cups, then stood.

Stephens interrupted Donald's expansive

speech. “You two taking off?”

“I need some air, Daddy. Andy’s going to walk with me.”

The older man looked at Andy. “Take care of her, Carrington.”

“Will do, sir.”

As Andy stepped outside, Lauren tucked her arm within his. Her tiny smirk told him all he needed to know. She’d gotten her way. He sighed. He didn’t want to hurt the girl. His aim had been to help her. But if she was determined to get his attention one way or the other, his choices of help narrowed the longer he was with her.

She gave his arm a little squeeze. “Where shall we stop first?”

“What happened to the short walk you wanted to take?”

“A few first class bar stops on the way won’t hurt anything.”

“I don’t bar hop. Not interested. Let’s walk and talk.”

She cuddled against him. “What shall we talk about?”

Andy eased a fraction away from her. “How about your interests?”

“What? Art? Good times? You want to hear about the clothes I like?”

“Do you like animals?”

“Daddy has this old, dilapidated dog who’s ancient and will never die. He’s smelly and temperamental, but Daddy refuses to put him down.” Lauren’s pert nose raised another notch into the air.

“Dilapidated?” Andy laughed. “What kind of dog?”

The look she leveled at him was full of confusion. "Beats me. I think he's some kind of hound."

"Ain't nothing but a hound dog." Andy sang under his breath.

"What? What do you mean?"

Caroline would have understood at once. That was one thing that bonded his friends together. A love of oldies—cars and songs.

"It was nothing. Just me, being ridiculous." He shook his head. "You don't own a pet?"

"I always wanted some fish."

"Why fish?"

"I don't know. Maybe because I love the water, love watching them in their habitat, swimming carefree and gracefully." Her cheeks reddened. "Promise you won't laugh if I tell you something?"

"Never."

"When I was a kid I dreamed of being a mermaid and living forever in the water. I'd only come out long enough now and then for two-legged humans to admire me." Lauren laughed. "Isn't that stupid?"

"I think it's cute." Andy patted her hand resting on his arm. "Someday, you'll make the right man a wonderful wife."

"Why not you?"

"Not me. You'd be tired of me and my in-sophistication in a week's time."

The pout on her face gave him a momentary twinge of sorrow, but Caroline's expressive face refused to leave his memory or heart. He could no more forget the girl he'd loved forever than he could forget to breathe. As lovely as Lauren was, there would never be anyone but Caroline for him.

Probably hopeless. Linc had claimed her attention.

"I don't suppose you'd want to take a boat out past Lady Liberty, would you? I've never seen her. Might as well get some sightseeing in."

Interest sparked in her eyes. "I love boating at night. Sure, let's go."

"You know what and where to go, I assume?"

"Leave it to me."

Lauren did, indeed, know where to go. The boat they boarded was nearly empty. She arranged for a couple of guys with string instruments to play while they sailed, and Andy almost backed out. He suspected well enough what Lauren was scheming.

It was a warm night, and the shore lights were bright and gorgeous. Andy wished he'd brought a sketchpad. He followed her to the back of the boat where they leaned on the rail and enjoyed the sea breeze.

What would Caroline be doing tonight? He'd not called and told her he'd be away nearly all week, hoping she'd wonder and miss him. Was she with Linc? At home, messing around in the shop or whipping up one of her quirky meals?

Someday he'd do a whole series of paints with her as the subject. Curled up on the sofa reading. In the kitchen with a smudge of flour on her nose. The possibilities were endless.

With a sudden mood switch, depression swamped him, and he wondered if he was fooling himself. She gave no indication she'd ever change her mind about him. Was he wrong?

His groan came from deep within his heart. *God, you know...*

Lauren's pensive face stood out against the darker night. What was she thinking about? Him? Or something more personal? Her earlier words returned now.

See what an influence you are on me.

He suspected she was not only spoiled and hungry for attention, but for something to make a difference in her life.

"It's a beautiful night."

Lauren glanced around as if his words had just made her aware of the world around her.

"Y-e-s. I guess." She leaned sideways and laid her head on his shoulder, and then swayed as the boat rode through a rough wave.

When Andy touched her back to steady her, she turned and wrapped her arms around him. Her head tilted back and she stared into his face. "Andy, oh, Andy."

Her eyes shimmered with what looked like tears. Her lips trembled. "Please hold me, Andy. Just for a minute."

She rested that way for a moment, then almost as if mesmerized, she lifted her head to gaze into his eyes again. Her lips parted and she leaned forward—lovely and tempting. "Kiss me? Please?"

Her appealing face could have been inviting. He wondered at life. For another person, she would be the perfect match. Here was a girl who'd let it be known she could and would care for him if he'd say the word. And Caroline—the girl who held his heart captive—disdained his love.

He gently pushed her away. “You’re a tempting morsel, Lauren Stephens.”

“That’s the first time anyone’s said that to me.” Her laugh was light and long.

“It’s true nevertheless.”

“Just not tempting enough.”

“That's true too, but we can still be friends, for sure.”

It was her turn to sigh. “Why aren’t you engaged if you care so much for the girl in West Virginia?”

Her question wasn't funny, but he laughed anyway. “Because she doesn’t care for me.”

Lauren’s incredulous look widened his mouth even more.

“What? I can’t believe that. She’s—”

“Careful, that’s my girl you’re talking about.”

“Even though technically she isn’t your girl.” Lauren’s moue was full of frustration. “Why doesn’t she care for you?”

“Perhaps she knows me too well. Could be I’m not famous enough or rich enough.”

“You’re kidding, I hope.”

Was he? Not entirely. “Well, let’s just say, everyone has dreams.”

“It’s just a matter of time before both of those things happen—now that Daddy’s involved. Can’t she see your potentiality?”

“I don’t know what Caroline sees. Her brother’s my best friend. A guy she grew up with. A man who’s not been too successful so far.” Andy grinned down at the pint-sized girl beside him.

“Let’s do something about it.”

“I’m working on the successful part—”

“That’s not what I’m talking about.”

"What then?"

"Jealousy. We'll make her jealous."

"I don't know. That kind of thing has a tendency to backfire." Andy shook his head. "She already has her eye on Lincoln Tillis."

Lauren brushed away the fine spray blowing up from the water below. "The tall dark guy. I met him, remember?"

"What do you have in mind?" Andy leaned on the rail and stared down into the water. "Nothing too drastic, I hope?"

"You can trust me." Lauren patted his arm. "Call your best friend. Toby, isn't it?"

"Is there something important I need to tell him?"

"Yes. Tell him you're on a boat with romantic music in the background and me right beside you." Lauren dimpled.

Andy punched in Toby's number. "And how's that supposed to help?"

"You'll see." Lauren whirled in a circle. "By the time we get back to West Virginia, your girl will know we've spent days together."

"You minx."

"My motives may be in question, but my methods are very effective."

When Toby answered, Andy said, "How are things going?"

"Good. We're still in Charleston. Heard about a couple of other auctions that sounded too good to miss."

"Both there?"

"No. One's on down in Virginia. I'm still debating whether to be away from the shop that long or not. That will be two weeks away, and I've seldom stayed away that long."

"I'm sure Caroline can handle it."

"Sure she can. She may not like it though. What are you up to?"

"I'm still in New York seeing the sights. Lauren's a perfect guide. In fact, we're on a boat now drifting past New York's shoreline with music in the background."

Toby grunted. "Romantic. I thought—"

"You thought right. Lauren and I are only friends." Andy hastened to assure his friend of his devotion to Caroline.

"Just be careful. I'd hate to have to break your neck if you hurt Sis."

"If I remember correctly I've had to use the same line on you more than once."

"A little teasing never hurt any sister," Toby objected. "When are you headed home?"

He wouldn't admit it to even his best friend, but the first stirrings of lonesomeness tugged at his heart. What were sights without the girl he loved by his side? Donald and Lauren both had urged him to stay for a few days to see the sights. But all he wanted right now was home and Caroline.

"Tomorrow. I'm flying back in the morning." The leap of his spirits assured him his spur-of-the-moment decision was the right one. He ignored Lauren's startled look. "I'm anxious to get to work again."

Toby's chuckle came through the phone. "See ya soon."

Andy slipped his cell in his pocket and motioned to the captain of the tour boat. Lauren grabbed his arm.

"What are you doing? You promised to stay for a few days."

"I've changed my mind."

"I can't get ready to leave by morning."

"Then if you really want to come back, do so when you can. I need to get home."

"But what about our plan?" Her pout told him she wasn't pleased with the change of plans.

"Your plan? If you come to Appleton, we'll see how it plays out."

Lauren's chatter was background noise as they sailed back to the harbor. He stared at the beautiful city lights, his heart warm, his heart leaping ahead of his body.

He was going home.

Chapter Sixteen

Caro held onto the rail as she descended the stairs.

She'd found, earlier in the day, the heels she'd bought in the very back of her closet and looked at them in horror. Why on earth had she purchased the things?

I must have been out of my mind.

She'd sat down on the floor and slipped them on, stretched out her leg to examine it. Not too bad. She twisted her ankle. At least she had slim ankles. Maybe—if she could learn to walk in them—she would be okay.

Now, though her ankles had a tendency to wobble, she didn't think she was doing too bad a job of walking in them. But she wouldn't take chances and tightened her grip on the rail.

The doorbell rang. Caro hurried to answer the door, flung it open, and nearly swooned.

Crease lines appeared between Linc's eyes. He stretched out a hand. "Are you all right?"

"I'm fine. You're so stunning, you took my breath away."

"You crazy girl. I thought you were having a heart attack. Anyhow, that's supposed to be my line."

He stood back and studied her, then lifted his gaze to meet hers. "You're beautiful."

She opened her mouth to refute his statement, then snapped it shut. If he thought so, why enlighten him? With a grin, she motioned him to enter.

"Let me check for any last minute messages, then I'll be ready." She hit the message button and waited. Toby's voice came on.

"Hey, sis, how's it going? Making lots of money for my retirement?" A laugh. "Andy called last night. You did know he's in New York, didn't you? Hanging around some big shots the way I hear it. Remember the red-head I told you about?"

How could she forget? Was that girl the only thing Appleton could talk about?

"She and Andy are having a blast in New York. Sightseeing. Trying out new restaurants. She lives there so she's showing him around. Got her sights set on our Andy, I'd say. Gotta go. Just thought I'd touch base, but you must be out—and—about."

Her fingers curled in agony. Why did Toby have to call right now? For that matter, why did he think she would care what Andy did? She hit the erase button and spun away from the machine.

"I'm ready."

"This is for you. To celebrate our first official date." Linc handed her a variegated pink and white orchid. His action was lovely, his manner breathtakingly polite, but were his eyes searching her face a little too much? He couldn't have helped but hear Toby's taunting message.

"It's gorgeous. Thanks." Caro pinned them to her shoulder, then locked the shop door as they left.

Taking her elbow, he guided her to his vehicle. Caro wanted to stretch out a hand to scoop up her suddenly-dragging spirits. Andy and the trouble he caused her.

Linc's SUV was big and luxurious. Caro ran a hand over the plush leather seat. Roomy and not at all like Andy's bug where two people in the front almost rubbed shoulders. But then it was kind of cozy in Andy's bug, especially when it rained.

"Do you like the leather?"

"It's divine."

"You look pensive. What are you thinking?"

"I was just thinking about Andy's bug and comparing it to this big SUV. It's cozy during showers, but not very comfortable."

"Great little economical cars. I had one myself during college. Hated giving it up, but when I became a family man, I needed something bigger. Besides in West Virginia a person needs something that'll maneuver the mountains during winter."

The silence in the vehicle grew.

"Are you okay?"

"I was thinking about Andy's thefts." Including him, New York, and Lauren Stephens. And the list she'd found in his SUV.

"His pictures? You haven't found out who's involved, have you?"

"I can't help but wonder about his neighbor, Gerald Bennett." Caro went on to explain for the twenty-minute ride to Charleston, about the man's strange behavior that afternoon when she'd talked with him. "He has to be hiding something. I'm sure of it."

"Maybe not. Could be he's just naturally nosy, but tried to foist off your questions because you caught him at it."

"Maybe." She thought about Mr. Bennett and had to concede he'd probably be the type to dislike people prying into his business while feeling it was his privilege to nose a little in others'.

After he parked, they walked together into the lobby of the restaurant. She touched his arm. "Is there a phone I could use? I left my cell at home."

"Sure." Linc led her to a private corner where a phone sat on a small table hidden discreetly by a large live plant. He started to walk away. "I'll be right over there."

"Stay if you want." Caro punched in Andy's cell number. "I thought of something and want Andy to check it out."

His answering machine clicked on.

"Andy, its Caro. I thought of something. Did you think to ask Stephanie or Mr. Bennett if they'd seen a red Camaro? She didn't say when we talked with her and Bob. Remember? Anyhow, I think you ought to check it out. Call me when you can, and we'll talk more about it."

She hung up, her thoughts on the man she'd just called. Where was he? Out romancing Cute Red Head? Linc stirred beside her, and she beamed up at him. "I'm glad I thought of that. I hope he checks it out."

Linc touched her back as they followed the maître d' to their table. When they'd settled and ordered their sparkling white grape juice, Linc spoke. "You're really serious about this detecting business."

Caro stuffed the last vestiges of Andy's image into the recesses of her mind and nodded. "I am. I always thought I'd like to try my hand at it. Loved mystery and suspense books growing up. I enjoyed pitting my wits against the writer's ability to keep the bad guy unknown."

"I can see that."

"But most of all, I can't stand to think someone will get away with stealing Andy's pictures. I don't particularly like them, but they must have something, cause everyone else who sees them adores them."

Linc leaned forward and sipped at his drink while eyeing her. "And he's a good friend."

Was he jealous? If her memory wasn't taking a nap, they'd already had this conversation. "He's my brother Toby's best friend. But I've known him all my life. He's like a brother to me."

"You did mention that."

What was this man thinking? Was he consumed with thoughts about her? Did he really like her and was he interested? She'd never thought in a hundred years someone like him would come along—even if she had dreamed and hoped for it to happen.

His eyes were so serious and intent, and she liked the way he styled his dark hair. Short, with just a fashionable bit of tangled-ness on top. Caro drew in a quick breath.

When his slow words came, it was as if he was still pondering what he would say. "No. I'm thinking that's not quite right."

What were they even talking about? She'd totally forgotten. "What do you mean?"

"Do you know what we've talked about all evening?"

Her heart sank. She'd dominated the talk about herself and bored him stiff. She reached for, then sipped from the crystal glass, and let her fingers tighten around it before setting it down again on the while tablecloth. "I'm sorry. I didn't mean to be so hoggish with the conversation. Did I bore you too badly talking about myself?"

Linc reached across the table and took her hand. "Caro, you didn't bore me. I want to hear about you."

"Then ...?"

"You're so obsessed with Andy Carrington he's all you talk about. And don't get me wrong. I don't mind, per se. I like the energetic way you speak about your friends. But a little less Carrington and a little more Caro Gibson would be very interesting to me."

Was her face flushing as red as the heat in her cheeks felt? How could she be so ignorant? She had to make him understand. She wasn't in love with Andy. She wanted...

What did she want?

Linc? Then she'd better straighten up and fly right.

"I'm sorry. I do have a tendency to fixate on whatever—or whomever, in this case—that is presently consuming my life. I'll be more careful. Tell me about yourself." There. That should make him forget her gaff. Didn't men like to talk about themselves?

Her cheeks burned even more as she remembered her own carefree words, caught up in her own thoughts and world. "What do you do? I mean, besides your work at church?"

His eyes still held a trace of reserve in them,

the warmth from before hovering on the edges of his emotional restraint. "I dabble in several different things but also own a couple radio stations—one in Clarksburg which is easy listening and a gospel in Charleston—hence my interest in the drama ministry at our church. In fact, I thought you might be interested in viewing a rehearsal we're doing later this evening?"

"I'd love it. But won't that make it awfully late for you?"

"I've got business here tomorrow and can stay over, or I can get you a room if you'd rather drive back in the morning." He raised an eyebrow. "Besides, I'd like you to meet the kids."

Beyond him, two tables away, a beautiful, dark-haired woman sat staring. Caro blinked. Maybe the beauty knew Linc. She certainly didn't know her.

"Are you directing the play?"

"My assistant will be in charge tonight. But I thought we could drop in so they'd know there's no such thing as lax practices."

The woman beckoned, and a waiter appeared immediately. She spoke, her hand reaching up to twist a strand of her hair. He nodded and left.

Caro focused on Linc again. "Do you plan on acquiring more stations?"

"Definitely. I'm in the process of negotiating for another, but it's out of state. And I have my eyes on a couple of others."

"Really? I'm impressed. Does it take much of your time?"

"Not really. I have excellent employees who

do most of the work."

"And what about your son? Is he interested in taking over your business some day?"

"Well, I hope that's a good many years down the road. He's got a business head so perhaps. We'll see when he gets a bit older."

The waiter who'd spoken with the brunette appeared at their table. Caro looked up, but the man stared at Linc who cocked his head in question.

"Excuse me, sir. The lady behind you asked me to give this to you." He discreetly slipped a paper into Linc's hand.

For just a second, Caro's date stared at the folded paper, then he turned half way around.

The woman smirked, her eyes sending messages straight to Linc.

Caro wanted to bite down on something hard to vent the frustration eating at her. "How big is your church?"

Linc shifted back around, his face unsmiling and grim. "Last time I heard, they have around five hundred members. For this area, that's a good size."

Good. At least she'd gotten his attention again. The woman beyond their table frowned, stood and headed to the door, but halfway there, she swerved and stopped at their table.

"Have you thought about what we talked about?"

"Too busy. Not sure I'm interested."

"Don't wait too long. I have others who'll jump at the chance to make the bucks." She tossed the words at Linc as she turned to stroll away.

Who was she? Caro did her own frowning

when she caught Linc's gaze resting on the fashionable figure sauntering out. Should she ask him or ignore the whole situation?

Ignore. Definitely.

"It is. Ours is much smaller, but I love Pastors Haag and Scott and the church people. I've known most of them all my life, and they're some of the best in the country." Caro enthused, then remembered she needed to focus on her date.

"Would you like to attend one of our Sunday services some time?"

No, she wouldn't. Caro barely kept herself from wincing. She hated to be away from her own church on Sundays, hated to travel, hated new and different things that made her feel more awkward than she already was.

She looked at Linc's eager face and knew there was no way she wanted to hurt him. She couldn't afford to. Not if she was interested in being the next Mrs. Tillis.

"Maybe. I teach the youth at my own church, so I'm not sure when I could get away."

"I see."

What did he see? She stretched out an arm and touched his hand that lay on top of the table. "But I'm willing to work something out so I can."

Forty-five minutes later, they left the restaurant, and headed toward Clarksburg. When Linc pulled into an impressive parking lot of a large brick and glass church, Caro hoped her mouth hadn't fallen open. Linc tucked her hand in the crook of his arm and led her to a large auditorium styled building.

"You know, don't you, I'm showing you off?"

"Are you?" Caro looked over her shoulder and motioned to the gigantic church. "I'm in awe. I'm not sure I should enter such an impressive structure. Do I have stars in my eyes?"

He leaned down and stared into her eyes.

The moment lengthened, and Caro held her breath. What was he thinking?

Then slowly he straightened and took one of her hands. "No, afraid not. We're just people here, Caro. The same as your smaller church you love so well. We'll check in on the cast, then I'll show you our church. Relax. You'll enjoy this."

Linc settled her into a seat where she had a good view, then strode toward the front, where the current on-scene actors faltered. He waved them to continue and stood in front of the stage.

Watching the crew practicing their summer production was a lesson in amateur professionalism. When they'd finished the scene, they gathered around him. He held up a hand until they quieted then spoke in a voice that carried to the back of the room where Caro sat.

"Caro, come meet my friends."

She gripped the armrest for a second, then stood, swallowing. *Lord, don't let me fall on my face.*

Float. *Float.* Caro slowed her walk and tried to visualize Andy's demonstration on floating. The thought was a happy one and eased the tension, and when she reached the group clustered around the good-looking director, he met her eyes and matched her grin.

Clasping her hand, he pulled her close. "Caro, these are the scoundrels I have to work with when we get ready for a play."

Laughs and hoots greeted his teasing. Caro let her gaze wander from person to person.

"I'm not even going to try to tell you all their names..." He turned back to the group. "...but this is a very special person. This, my friends, is the famed Caroline Gibson. The playwright of the last two Christmas plays we did. And, she's agreed to write our next one exclusively for us."

A surge of excitement ripped through her. Her dreams were coming true. A handsome, attentive man who gave every indication things could become a lot more serious between them, and a touch of fame that set very well. She loved all of it.

She only had to remember to stay off the subject of Andy Carrington.

Chapter Seventeen

It ended up being a two-day outing.

Caro shut out her brother's accusing eyes and haunting voice in her mind when they began to play over and over. She knew she shouldn't leave the shop closed, but she couldn't resist Linc's suggestions.

After all, Toby didn't think twice about taking off a couple days—or more—every month. Why shouldn't she have an outing? Especially an important one like this. Caro refused to think about the job description they'd both agreed upon. There would be time enough to worry about it later.

Caro took another turn around the spacious hotel room Linc had rented for her, bounced once on the humongous four poster bed, then nibbled on a chocolate. This was the life. If Toni and Starli could see her now. She giggled.

In the bathroom she ran a tub full of water, tossing in half a bottle of the complimentary bath salts. But before she could enjoy its relaxing warmth, the hotel phone rang. Who would be calling this time of the night? She lifted the receiver and spoke into it.

Toni DeLuca-Douglas' voice came through the receiver. "Caro, where are you? Toby gave me the hotel phone number."

"In Clarksburg. Linc wanted me to see his church's new play they're practicing. Tomorrow morning we're stopping at his radio stations, then a couple hours at his church while he directs play practice, and tomorrow night we're eating dinner with his two kids."

"He has two children?"

Was that reservation in Toni's voice?

"Y-es. Is that a problem?"

"Of course not. You know I love Blake like he was my own."

Toni's stepson was an adorable twelve-year-old who she doted on. Caro knew if anyone would understand, Toni would.

"I'm kind of nervous meeting them. What if they don't like me?"

"This sounds serious. You must really like Linc to care that much about what his children think."

Caro hesitated. "I do. I like Linc a lot."

"I wouldn't worry. You do so well with our young people at church. They adore you."

"Yeah." Caro drawled out the words. "Because I'm crazy enough to try anything they want to do."

Toni's soft laugh made Caro's lips tilt up.

"True. But you're also a great example for them. Not too preachy, but enough influence to keep them in line."

"I love working with them."

"We all know that. I wouldn't worry. Linc's children will love you."

A comfortable silence settled between them.

"I called—"

"Why did—"

Caro chuckled at their mutual statements at the same time. "Did you call for a reason or did you just want to hear my voice? Miss me, do you?"

"I wanted to tell you Andy called the other night. He's in New York, you know, on business. I guess Lauren is showing him the town."

The stab of pain that pierced her heart hurt worse than a toothache. "If he went for business, how does he have time to see *her*?"

"She's a lovely girl."

Was Toni being disloyal to *her*? "But tricky."

"Why do you think that?"

"She's after Andy, and he can't see it."

"So? Andy's a very eligible man. Any woman who gets him will be making a smart move."

Caro squeezed her eyes shut in agony. How could Toni say this? "I'm just thinking of Andy."

"Well, Andy needs someone who will adore him. Someone who loves art and appreciates his work."

Ouch. Toni was laying it on pretty thick today.

"Meaning, I don't."

"You don't want him. Why should you care who gets him?"

Touché.

Once again, Andy's face flashed in her mind. The way he'd cock his head as he listened to her talking about a subject. Not at all like Toby's I-could-care-less attitude. The way he had always looked back to check on her when he and Toby, with her tagging along behind, had headed to a favorite playing spot. But why think of that now?

"I don't want him hurt." Caro heard the sulkiness in her voice and tried to cover it up with a grin. She knew she'd failed when she heard Toni's gentle sigh.

"I wanted you to know. Talk later, okay?" Toni said and hung up.

Why had Toni called? She hadn't shared anything important.

Unless Andy being with Lauren was important.

~*~

Linc picked her up at eight sharp the next morning.

"Hungry?"

"Starved."

"I know this place that has the best pancakes. And their sausage is great, too."

Calories. But for once, she'd splurge. Her stomach growled in anticipation.

Her hand tucked within his, they walked inside. His fingers were long and firm. She liked the feel of them threaded through her own. He paused just inside the door. "Booth or table?"

"Booth, of course."

They scooted side by side into one of the booths near the back of the restaurant and a waitress slapped down menus.

"We want pancakes, Marie." Linc gave his menu a shove back toward her. "With apples and plenty of cream filling."

"I'm regretting this already. I'll have to walk ten miles to work it off."

"You're thin as a rail. A few pancakes won't hurt you."

Did he mean she was skinny? Caro cringed. Toby and Andy had teased her without mercy about her skinny legs when they were kids.

The pancakes were delicious. She ate half of hers before shoving the plate away. "I can't eat another bite. Can I take them home with me?"

"You won't want them. The crew always orders calzones for lunch when we practice on Saturdays."

"I'm not eating another bite till supper."

"We'll see about that. I'll be right back."

She watched his long-legged stride and felt her stomach turn over. He was a walking ad for those clothes. Propping her chin on her fist, she allowed herself the daydream of being married to Lincoln Tillis.

Only the sense that someone stood at her elbow drew her out of the vision. She glanced up.

The waitress—Caro peered at the woman's nametag to refresh her memory—leaned against the back of the seat.

"Did you need something, Marie?"

"May I sit down a minute?"

"Well—sure."

"You really like Linc, do you?" Marie tucked her order pad inside her pocket, slipped the pencil behind her ear, and sat. "Do you know Linc has other girlfriends?"

"What?" Could the woman in the restaurant last night be one of them? If her heart sunk any lower it would touch her toes. No way could she compete with gorgeous females like that.

"Since his wife died, he's gone with four different women."

"And you're telling me this because...?" He was handsome and probably financially stable. Was it so strange for an eligible widower to date?

But *four* women? He couldn't have been serious over any of them.

What about her? Was he playing with her? She pictured the sincerity in his dark eyes. No, she didn't think so. She hoped not.

She eyed the woman across from her. Was that a malevolent glint in her eyes? What was her purpose in telling her this?

Whether Linc ever proposed, he was serious in his affection right now. Caro didn't doubt that.

"Who were these women?" Might as well find out all she could.

A shrug as if it didn't matter. "You wouldn't know them."

"Maybe. Maybe not. But I can ask Linc who they are." Caro bit the inside of her jaw. Did she really want to go there?

"I wouldn't. It would be too embarrassing."

"Not for me." Marie's objection made her the more determined to find out the truth. "Tell me. I want to know."

Marie pressed her lips into a firm line. "I can tell you this, DeeDee Reynolds is hurt. She thought he cared, and now, he's dropped her for—you."

"What does DeeDee look like?" Caro narrowed her eyes.

The woman smirked. "Much prettier than you."

Not much of a feat. "Describe her please."

"Dark brown, wavy hair, well-built but dresses fantastic. She has a habit of fiddling with her hair when she talks."

Definitely the woman from last night. She

must still be after Linc. Ugh. "I don't want to cause—"

"You'd better watch out for him."

"Is that a warning?" Caro wouldn't have been surprised to see her shake a finger in her face. "There comes Linc now. Let's face him with this."

"Mind what I said." The waitress jumped to her feet, then bent down to whisper. "Don't say anything. Run while you can."

"Marie."

The waitress paused.

"Why are you so interested in Linc's love life?"

The waitress's eyes grew cold. She shook her head, and trotted back to the counter.

Caro turned to Linc as he approached.

"Ready to go?" Linc pulled out his wallet and tossed five-dollars on the table.

The man who'd been such a gentleman to her paid the bill, smiling and joking a little with the cashier. She'd never seen him act anyway but courteous to all who crossed his path.

"We'll make a quick stop at the station here in town, then if you'd like I figured we'd spend the rest of the morning at the church as they practice." He started the SUV. "After lunch, I thought you might like to see some local sights."

"And tonight?" She was nervous about his kids, but him? Definitely looking forward to another evening with him.

"I told the kids we'd pick them up around seven. I've made reservations at the Oak Ridge Club House. Excellent food. You'll enjoy it."

"Your children know about me?" Another spasm of nervousness spread through her stomach.

"I don't try to hide my dates from them."

Dates? At least he wasn't hiding information from her.

"You're not nervous, are you? They're not ogres, you know."

"Of course not. I didn't think that."

The quiet in the SUV would have lulled her to sleep if she hadn't been pondering the best way to bring up all the girls Marie had said he'd dated.

It wasn't any of her business, but she couldn't stand not knowing. If he was flighty, she had a right to know. She had a right to know whether he considered her more than just a date.

But he hadn't asked her who she'd dated.

Good grief, he was good looking. "Linc?"

"Yes, d—Caro?"

Had he almost said another woman's name? The fascinating DeeDee he'd supposedly discarded, according to Marie? "Have you dated a lot of women?"

"What brought about that question?" His lips tilted up. "What's bothering you?"

This wasn't as hard as she'd thought it would be. "Marie—"

His smile morphed into a frown. "From the restaurant?"

"Yes. While you were gone she let me know you'd gone with a lot of girls and to watch out."

His explosive burst of laughter was the best medicine to cure her doubts.

"Meaning to be careful around me? That I'm

untrustworthy?"

"Yes. She said you broke DeeDee Reynolds' heart."

"DeeDee was—is—" His lips pressed together. Had his face grown a shade redder than before? Embarrassment? Anger? "Do you believe Marie?"

"No-o-o. I don't really know. I don't want to."

"That doesn't sound convincing." He pulled into a parking lot and shut off the engine. "We need to talk, but not now. Come on."

"But, I—"

"Not now, Caro." His left hand gripped the steering wheel, knuckles white as he stared down. Then he spoke—his voice strained with the effort to speak normally. "I can't tell you—. There's things—I can't—I'm not at liberty to talk about. You'll have to trust me, Caro. For now."

Caro followed Linc into the station. He'd told her nothing, but she sensed he was disturbed. Had Marie's accusations bothered him more than he wanted her to know? And what were all the hints and unfinished sentences about?

~*~

The station was fun to watch. Caro enjoyed gazing through the window at the DJ working his magic. He gave Linc and her a nod while the music played and slipped out of his headgear to pop outside the door for a minute.

"How's everything going?" Linc nodded at Caro. "My friend from Appleton. How about playing something special for her?"

"Sure. What would you like to hear?" The grinning DJ tapped fingers on the door jam.

"I don't know." Caro responded to his

friendliness with a grin of her own. "I can't think. Wait. I love 'You Are So Beautiful.'"

"Gotcha. See ya, boss."

"No. Not that one." He spoke casually, but his tone held an edge of tightness. "Play 'It's A Wonderful World.' How's that, Caro?"

Caro wouldn't have minded so much, but the nagging thought her choice had meant something special to Linc, and the specialness didn't have anything to do with her, buzzed in her mind like a gnat. What other woman in his life had loved that song?

They stayed long enough for Caro to hear her song and for Linc to check with his business manager, then left for the church.

Linc seemed to have forgotten their earlier conversation. Caro suspected he might not bring it up again.

"The cast is having some problems with some of the scenes. A few spots seem kind of rushed—jerky, maybe—but no one can figure out what the problem is. Would you keep an ear peeled?"

"I'd love to, Linc. Do you have an extra script so I can follow along?" Caro shifted in her seat and tucked a leg under herself.

"Sure. Remind me to get you one."

She waited on him to say more, but his gaze remained glued to the road ahead. Sighing, she readjusted her body and joined Linc in staring out the windshield.

Chapter Eighteen

Caro settled into a seat mid-way of the auditorium and allowed her eyelids to close. Linc had barely spoken to her for the last half-hour.

True, he no doubt had the practice on his mind. But still...She wasn't used to guys like this.

What was she used to? Mild-mannered teases like Toby—and Andy. She twisted her mouth into a grimace.

What had Linc had on his mind when he'd vetoed her song selection? A woman? *What* woman? DeeDee Reynolds? For that matter, why had his face been so grim when he'd spotted her in the restaurant? And that note from her. Obviously, he wasn't planning to tell her the contents.

Linc stood with several of the cast surrounding him. He cast a glance over his shoulder, then called out.

"Caro, it's at the end of the first scene."

She lifted a hand, but didn't speak. If he wanted to ignore her, she wouldn't be the first one to break the silence. *I need to be mature here, to know what I'm was up against if I'm going to be...well, maybe the next Mrs. Tillis.*

His gaze was questioning when he looked at her again, but he said nothing, only broke away from the others and strode to her. She almost wilted in relief. Now, he would take her hand and make up for ignoring her.

"Caro?"

She jumped to her feet. "What, Linc?"

"I wanted to show you the spot on your script so you'd be sure to catch it."

"I'd rather catch it without your help. If it's so troublesome, I'll not have any problem." Caro peered at him, but his gaze shifted away. Her heart sank. He wasn't going explain about his sudden moodiness.

She drew in a deep breath and took the plunge. "Linc, I didn't mean to upset you with Marie's accusations. You don't have to explain yourself to me." So much for playing it cool.

His gaze swiveled back to her, his features relaxed and at ease again. "I'm not angry with you, Caro. I am upset. I'll tell you about it later."

She doubted it.

His hand was strong, yet gentle when he squeezed hers. "Okay?"

Heart in her throat, she swallowed. "Okay."

He walked away, and with his back safely toward her, Caro admired his long legs then called after him. "I want to see the whole thing first, then we'll address the problem."

It was a two-hour play, but with the stops and starts, took almost three. She nodded at Linc when he glanced at her.

"Got it. Here's what I think." She walked forward and explained her ideas. "This scene where the primary actors are together doesn't set right. You—" Caro pointed at an actor. "—need to turn away from Trisha. You can't convey anger when you're looking longingly at her face. And the others need to step back so the focus is entirely on Trisha and John."

She looked at the cast. "Do you understand?"

At their nods, she said, "Start at the beginning again, and I'll stop you if it's no smoother."

She sat in the front row beside Linc and felt his touch when he reached for her hand. When the actors entered the awkward spot, they waltzed through it, and Linc squeezed her fingers softly.

Rising from his seat, Linc began clapping, and Caro joined in.

"That's perfect. Thank you, Caro."

"Glad to help."

"All right, guys, we're done for the day. Last practice next Tuesday. Give yourself a break over the weekend, then run over your lines Monday. I'll see you on Tuesday."

~*~

The dress fit like a glove. Cliché, but true. Caro twisted and viewed herself in the mirror, thankful that she'd thought to ask the maid about local dress shops. She'd sacrificed her two hours of rest to shop, and with the advice from a far-more-knowledgeable salesperson than herself, had bought this dress. Would Andy have approved her choice?

The lady had insisted it was perfect for her figure, and she could see why. The pale green brought out the green tints in her hazel eyes and almost made her forget the faint freckles adorning her nose.

"Well, this is as good as it's going to get for you, girl." Caro wrinkled her nose at her mirror-image. "So be it. Now go and remember to keep the talk centered on Linc."

The thought of his kids interrupted her thoughts. "You do okay with the kids at home. Why should these two be any different? Toni said, be yourself. Do it."

Her churning stomach objected to her admonition.

She whirled away. Enough criticism and advice. It was time to come up with what she could talk about with Linc and his offspring. She wished she'd asked him more questions about the two. Too late now. She'd have to wing it. Hopefully she'd keep her size seven-and-a-half-foot out of her mouth.

The discreet knock came right on time. Caro wiped her sweaty palms on the bedspread before answering.

Linc stood before her in a dark suit, his tangled curls, at least for the moment, tamed.

"Ready?"

"As much as I'll ever be."

"You're not still nervous, are you?"

She gave him a sideways glance. "What makes you think that?"

His grin nearly sent her heart in a tailspin.

"Your tight clutch on my arm clued me in."

"Sorry." She loosened her death grip.

"By the way, you look fantastic in that green."

She wondered what he'd do if she tilted her head and tossed out an old forties phrase, 'this ole rag?' but why rock the boat?

After they'd settled in his car, he said, "The kids got home late, but they should be ready by the time we get there."

Minutes later, Linc slowed, then pulled into

the drive of an elegant Cape Cod.

"It's beautiful, Linc."

"Not bad for this area. I'll be right back."

In two minutes he reappeared, locking and setting his security system. Where were his kids? Had they backed out? Good grief, they probably revolted against meeting her. Hated her name, her plays, and the thought that she was with their dad tonight.

He slid inside, started the SUV and backed out. "Mitsy picked them up. She's dropping them off."

"Who's Mitsy?"

"My sister. The kids love her and didn't want to wait on us. They'll meet us at the Club."

Yikes. It was true then. They didn't want to meet her and were postponing it to the very end.

When Linc turned onto the drive of the restaurant, Caro drew in her breath. The view was gorgeous, a sweeping, wide drive, green everywhere, landscaped into beautifully eye-catching scenery.

"I think you'd better take me home."

"No way."

"I'm sure to knock over a waiter or spill something on the nearest person. They'll escort me out for certain."

"Then I'll make sure I'm the person who gets splashed. You won't have to worry about any trouble."

"That's worse."

When they walked into the restaurant, Linc spoke to the maître d' and she led them toward a table close to a window that overlooked a large lake. Two teen-agers were already seated there.

Caro studied them as she walked across the floor beside Linc. The boy lounged in his chair, looking bored and sullen. He resembled his dad, although his body was stockier and probably shorter. The girl, slim like her father, had the same wavy hair, and would have been beautiful if the expression on her face hadn't spoiled her looks.

The huge grin on Linc's face expressed his pleasure at his kids' presence. Obviously he hadn't noticed their sulky expressions. Or else he planned to ignore them. He pulled out a chair for Caro.

"Thanks for coming, kidos. How's Mitsy?"

"Okay." The girl shrugged.

"Caro, this is Ashley and Dwight. Kids, my friend from Appleton, Caroline Gibson. She's the one who wrote our Christmas plays the last two years."

No enthusiastic response.

"Do either of you participate in the church's play productions?" Caro propped an elbow on the table and peered from one to the other. It wasn't too hard to catch the look they passed between them.

"Those boring—"

Linc's gaze rose from the menu he studied. "Ashley. You're talking to the playwright of those productions and my friend. Please show some respect."

"Sorry, dad," the girl apologized, insincerely, but still an apology. "No, I don't participate."

Great. Now what? "Dwight?"

"Nope. Too busy."

"Too busy taking apart anything he can find

to fix." His dad dryly commented, his gaze still perusing the menu.

"Are you into sports?" Anything to break the silence.

Dwight looked at her as if she'd grown an extra eye. "That's more Ashley's act. I'm a nerd."

"Nothing wrong with interest in computers and machines."

He didn't respond verbally, but his manner made it very clear he didn't care what she thought.

It went downhill from there. Mid-way through the meal, their waiter stopped by and informed Linc he had a telephone call.

Caro watched in dread as Linc excused himself and left her with his two children. Her gaze swiveled back Ashley. "You've got beautiful hair—"

The teen smirked. "You think you've got a chance with Dad?"

Caro's stomach tightened. She'd like to put these spoiled teens in their place. But what to say that wouldn't alienate Linc? She wanted a chance with Linc. Wanted Linc. Then she'd better watch her tongue. Diplomacy was called for.

"Who knows? Right now we're friends." She leaned forward and hoped to convey trust and sincerity to these two. "I'm sure you want him to enjoy himself. To have a life."

"He's got a life." Ashley snapped. "With *us*."

Caro's heart softened. "Of course, he does. You will always be in his heart. How could he forget you?"

"And Mom. He'll never forget her. He said

so."

For a long moment, Caro could only blink. "I'm sure your mother holds a very special place in his heart."

"First place in his heart, Miss Gibson." The fifteen-year-old snapped.

Dwight gave her a smug look. "Which you'll never be."

Maybe. Caro sat back and tried to relax even though she wanted to run from the room. All of a sudden she chuckled. She kept it up, paying no outward attention to the two teens, but saw them, from the corner of her eye. At first their sneers increased. Perplexity edged out the sneers, and at last, humor shone through. Dwight's lips twitched, and he slid a glance at his sister. Ashley's eyes widened, her hand flew to her mouth, and then she spluttered a laugh.

Yes. Caro's heart skipped a beat. When Linc's kids finally eased up on their laughing, Caro kept quiet, giving them a chance to speak first.

"What on earth are we laughing about?" Dwight choked out.

Ashley shrugged elaborately and snorted with laughter. "No idea. She's the one who started it."

Dwight grinned and turned to Caro. "What *is* so funny?"

"I was laughing at myself."

A puzzled look crossed both young faces. "What do you mean?"

"I tried the same thing years ago with my mother's boyfriends."

Ashley's face grew a little redder. "You mean—"

Caro took a long drink of her sparkling white grape juice. "My brother, Toby, and I were close to our parents. When dad died, Mom was devastated. For a long time, it was just the three of us. Gradually Mom and Toby accepted life had to go on, but I refused. The first five dates Mom had—"

"What?" Ashley and Dwight spoke together.

"I was such a brat, I scared every one of them off."

Ashley snickered. "How? Give us some tips."

"Whoa." Caro held up her hands in a slow-down motion. "Your dad won't appreciate me giving you guys more ways to run off his dates."

"Didn't work on you." Dwight offered. "Hey, dad, Caro's giving us some tips on how to—uh, discourage unwanted suitors."

Linc stood just behind her, his hand resting on her chair back. "She is, is she?" He put on a mock frown and sighed. "I wanted to see how far they got with you."

"You were in on this?" She couldn't believe it.

"Not exactly." Linc had the decency to look ashamed.

"Well?" she demanded, exasperation eating at her.

"They've pulled this on all the dates I've had with women I thought I could care for." Linc pulled out his chair and sat. "I figured you wouldn't be the exception."

She'd been had. She should have seen what was coming. "I suppose you let all your dates know what was going on?"

"No. Only you, and that's because you

passed the test."

"Test?" She sounded like a broken record.

"My kids figure if the women I date can stand their harassment, they can stand anything."

"And I passed this test?" How blind was she?

"With flying colors."

"I can't believe you bunch. How could you let them do this, Linc?" Caro stared from Linc's handsome face to the grinning faces of his children. She wanted to scowl at him, but his face registered so much mischief and fun at her, that her complaint seemed minor. Instead she glared for a second, then her lips twitched, and she joined in their laughter.

"We all like you, Caro." Linc touched her hand and rose. "Let's drop the kids off and take a spin around town."

Her heart thumped faster. Things were definitely looking up.

~*~

"Toni? How are you doing?" Andy leaned back in his office chair and cradled the phone between his shoulder and chin. "I've been trying to get a hold of Caroline. She's not answering their business phone, and you know how she's always forgetting her cell. Where on earth is she?"

Silence dragged through the line. Andy paused in fiddling with the sketches on his desk. "Toni?"

"Oh, dear. Andy, I hate to tell you this, but she's in Clarksburg." The distress in Toni's voice told him more than her words.

"Clarksburg? Is something wrong? Why is

she—" The reason hit him. "Oh."

"I tried to talk her out of it—sort of."

"Her idea or Lincoln's?"

"I don't know. Linc wanted her to meet his children, see his business, and I don't know what else." Toni hesitated. "It sounds serious, Andy. You've got to stop her."

All his happiness at being home was seeping out faster than water through a strainer. "I'm afraid she won't listen to me."

"She just doesn't realize what God wants, I'm sure."

"Maybe I've been wrong all along."

"Maybe, but I don't think so, Andy. You've got to hang in there. What if—?"

"What if what?"

"Did Lauren stay in New York?"

"Nope. She's at the hotel. Insisted on coming although I made it perfectly clear there would never be anything between us."

"You need something to attract Caro's attention. Would Lauren help us?"

"I'm sure she would. With what?"

"Let Caro see you and Lauren together."

"That won't be hard. Lauren's determined to capture what Caroline doesn't want in spite of my advice to the contrary." Andy studied the sketch he'd done of Caro on his way home. "When will she be home?"

"Tonight, I think. We'll be praying. Don't give up yet."

Andy tossed the phone down and scrubbed at his face. For the hundredth time in his life, Andy wasn't at all sure he'd win Caroline's heart.

Chapter Nineteen

The faint sound of the phone ringing penetrated through the closed door. Caro slipped her hand inside her handbag and dug for her keys.

When the phone quit ringing, then began again, she shoved her hand deeper into the bag and felt it slip from her grasp. It landed on the concrete, the contents scattering all over.

A groan escaped her lips, and she dropped to her knees. Linc dropped beside her.

"Relax. If it's someone who wants something important, they'll call back. You do have an answering machine?"

Caro raked a small tablet, pen, and peppermint drops toward herself. "Yes. But it might be..." Just in time she stopped.

Linc did not want to hear about Andy. She needed to remember that. She needed to forget Andy and his problems. Period.

"Might be who?"

"No one. I mean...no one important." That wasn't right either. Yikes. How did she get herself into these messes?

Lord, I thought you promised to guide us? Why am I always getting into trouble?

From the outside lights, Caro could see the twinkle in Linc's eyes when he paused and studied her. "Are you positive you didn't think it was Andy?"

What now? "I'm sorry, Linc. It's just I'm such a gung ho person. When I get interested in someone's problems or a project, I can't do it half way. I'm an all or nothing person." Caro looked at the man she so wanted to impress. Her heart beat with sudden intensity.

His face, partially shadowed, reflected an aura of mystery. But Caro could see the gentleness and interest lighten his features.

He moved a fraction closer. "You are. In the short time I've known you I've sensed that. It increases my interest in you. I like all or nothing."

A tom-tom pounded inside her chest. As if a magnetic field's forces were at work, Caro leaned forward. Her body shuddered.

Linc moved and in the porch light, she could see him clearly. His voice was a husky sound of awareness. "Caro..."

The sound of a car, the engine little more than a rippled gurgle, broke into her concentration. The screech of tires, the sound of a car door, and Caro turned her head. Who was it?

"Caro, is that you?"

Andy Carrington strode up the sidewalk, his thumbs in the pockets of khakis, looking so relaxed and Appleton-ish, her body relaxed at the sight, and then she jerked upright. What was she doing?

He stopped in back of them. "What are you guys doing? Hi, Linc. You guys just get back?"

The grouchiness settled in her mood like concrete hardening on the ground. To avoid Andy's intense stare, she scooped up another article belonging in her bag. "What are you doing here this late?"

She couldn't resist and lifted her gaze. Even in the spotty light, she saw an eyebrow lift.

"I tried to call you on my cell and when you didn't answer, I thought I'd drive by and see if you were still up. Did I interrupt you?"

Duh. "So it was you calling? I was trying to hurry and find my keys and dropped my bag."

"I see."

Andy said nothing as Linc and Caro finished gathering up the scattered items. When they stood, he made no move to leave, but followed them inside the business.

So much for a romantic ending to a date with Linc. Caro wanted to stomp across the floor. Andy had shown up at a very inopportune time. She wouldn't put it past him to be here to prevent it from happening.

But to be fair, how could he know when they'd get home, unless he'd been sitting somewhere waiting on their return? No way. He wouldn't do that, would he?

Would he? The thought was interesting. Did he care enough to keep her from a romantic evening with Linc? Caro sneaked a peak at Andy.

His gaze was on her, and almost as if he read her thoughts, he winked. Caro turned away.

He would! Those brown eyes of his gave him away.

"Well, since it looks like a party, let's go up to the apartment and have some coffee."

Caro led the way, the two men clomping behind her. Neither made any move to leave.

The door to the apartment stood open and

soft music drifted out. Caro stopped. She'd shut and locked the door, hadn't she? Or had she been in such a tizzy she'd forgotten?

"What's wrong, Caroline?" Andy stepped up on her right side.

Linc stepped up to her left. "Is something wrong?"

Caro leaned forward and peered inside the door, then with a shriek, she ran inside. "Toby, you're home. What did you buy? Where's Amy? I'm so glad you're back." She bent over the sofa and threw her arms around him.

Laughter covered his voice like chocolate coating a cherry. "When you quit smothering me, I'll explain." Caro felt his arms tighten around her and knew he was glad to see her.

When she'd released him, she put on her best provoked attitude. "I hate it when you go away."

"It's good for you." Toby leaned back on the sofa. "Makes you appreciate me more."

Caro perched on the arm. "Same old tease, aren't you? Will you never outgrow that?"

"Nope." Then he looked at the two men still standing by the doorway. "Who's your friend, Caro? Andy, what are you doing standing there like a statue? Since when did you quit calling this your second home?"

His face wreathed in a grin, Andy came over and swatted Toby on the shoulder.

"Toby, this is Lincoln Tillis from Clarksburg, the man I told you about who was interested in me writing a special play for his church."

"Caro and Linc just got back from a date."

Why was that piece of information pertinent right now? The glare she tossed at Andy went unnoticed as he refused to look at her.

"Oh, they did?" Toby looked from one to the other and grinned. "I hope you treated my sister with respect. I don't allow her to date without my permission, and I'm pretty particular whom she goes out with. You do have references, don't you?"

"That should be a required stipulation." Andy chimed in with his own undercover teasing.

"That's awful. How could you?" She lashed her brother with a daggering look, ignored Andy's two cents worth of comment, then appealed to Linc.

"Don't pay any attention to him. To either of them. They are awful. And when they're together, well, I bail out. There's no getting the best of them. Let me tell you, they were terrible to grow up with."

"I can imagine. Don't worry, Caro. I have two squabbling offspring, both determined to get the best of each other. And I grew up with three brothers and a sister."

Before she could comment that having three brothers was not quite the same as her situation, Linc spoke again. "No, I don't have references handy for you, but I'm glad you're taking my pursuit of Caro seriously."

Was that comment aimed at Andy? Bemusement definitely showed in those long-lashed eyes of Andy's. He'd gotten Linc's friendly warning.

And when had she begun noticing his lashes? Errgh. What was the matter with her? She needed to come to Linc's defense. Toby had no right to badger the man with his twisted humor.

"If you insist, you can call my church pastor. I'm sure he'll give you a glowing report of me. Anything to please the domineering guardian of a fair maiden."

Did Linc think this was a joke? He was egging her brother on. Toby would love that comment.

"And Linc favored the young people one evening with a speech."

Tattletale. Caro glared at Andy again. He was being mean to mention that flop of Linc's.

But Linc laughed again as if it was the joke of the century. "I tried to tell your sister I was no speaker. Give me a group to put together a rather good play, and I'm your man. But a speaker? Thanks, but no, thanks."

"You guys are hopeless. I give up. I'm going to get something to drink." She stood and looked at Linc. "And you're as bad as them."

Laughter followed her as she exited the room. Caro plugged in the coffeepot and measured the grounds. She considered digging out the package of cookies she'd bought recently, then vetoed the idea. They—those three buffoons—didn't deserve them.

A wonderful evening ruined. Well, not quite. It had been fun to meet Linc's cast of actors. She'd basked in the attention. And Linc had been exciting to be with, once she'd quit talking about Andy and his problems.

What would have happened out there on the stoop if Andy hadn't shown up when he did?

Would Linc have...kissed her? It had felt like it. His body language and vibes had said so. But would he have? Did he feel that way about her yet?

She looked up as Andy entered the kitchen. “Need some help?”

“Help? From you?” She sniffed.

He moved closer and placed an arm about her shoulders. “I’ll always be there to help you if you need it, don’t you know that?”

Friends again? She didn't think so. Not yet. “You interrupted a perfectly good evening. Then you come in here and point out stuff Toby does not need to know. How do you think Linc felt? He doesn’t know you guys like I do.”

Andy moved away, opened the fridge, peered in, then shut it. “Exactly. He needs to see what we’re like. See if he’s tough enough to take a little teasing. We don’t want you to hook up with a no-nonsense jerk.”

“That’s none of your's or Toby’s business, in spite of the yarn Toby was spouting in there.”

“Besides, I can’t ruin your evening. Only you—or Linc—can do that.” He swung around, stared at her for a moment, then headed for the other room. “I won’t apologize for showing up, Caroline. I’m glad I did. If my action interrupted your evening, too bad.”

He wasn’t sorry? He was glad he’d interrupted her evening—her romantic evening? He was trying to keep Linc and her apart. That’s what he was doing. She yelled at his back. “You spend days in New York with Lauren Stephens and then come home to ruin my chances of love?”

Andy disappeared back into their sitting room without a word. Caro fumed. But he was right. He couldn’t interrupt her relationship with Linc. She wouldn’t let him.

Forgetting about her decision to deny the men her cookies, she stacked them on a small platter, placed the cups and coffeepot on a tray and marched into the sitting room.

~*~

Linc explained his plans of acquiring the next radio station. Caro curled up on the end of the sofa and studiously kept her gaze from Andy's. She listened to the animated talk, unwilling and uninterested in participating. She let her gaze rest on Linc's handsome face.

What would it be like to be with this man for the rest of her life? A thought struck her. Would he expect her to move to Charleston? Uh, oh. She wouldn't like living in a big city like that. Visiting was one thing. Living there, another. And Clarksburg was way too far away. She wouldn't be able to stand it so far away from home.

Maybe they could get a house between Appleton and Clarksburg. The drive wouldn't be bad for either of them.

But would he want her to quit working at Undiscovered Treasures and help him in the radio business? Yuck. Her working as a DJ? Oh, yeah. That would be a blast. She'd have half of the listening area mad at her with her outspoken tongue.

The chuckle exploded from her, and three heads turned in her direction.

"You're laughing at Linc's plans?" Andy grinned at her, lights of delight causing his pupils to shine.

"I'd be offended if your laugh wasn't so beautiful."

Toby's eyes narrowed. "What's going on in

that mind of yours? You're not listening to us, are you?"

She didn't have to have a mirror to know her face was as red as an apple. Better get them off-track. "Nothing. Andy, you never did tell us why you stopped by?"

A hand lifted and ran through his sun-streaked blond hair. His whole face lit up. "I haven't, have I? But first, I have something I need to tell you, Tobe, old friend. I no longer am your best friend. Get that? Don't ever call me that again."

The humorous, confused look Toby turned on his life-long friend showed he understood Andy's words as well as Linc did. Which was not at all.

But Caro knew. Her mind flashed back to the bold statement she'd spouted to Andy.

I don't date Toby's friends.

If she hadn't known three pairs of eyes would have turned in her direction, she'd have patted her chest to get some air into her lungs. Instead she tried and failed to stop the advance of the red army of hot blood that surged to her cheeks again.

Andy Carrington had just knocked down her "supposedly" main excuse to not date him. He thought. She'd have to rack her brain for another excuse. Besides, what about Lauren Stephens?

That stiffened her spine. She cast him an iron-clad smirk for good measure. He couldn't buffalo her. They were not a couple and were not meant to be. No way.

Why, she wouldn't go with him *anywhere even* if he bribed her.

Backing against the fireplace, Andy interrupted her rebellious thoughts. "I've just signed a contract with Stephen Stephens. He's a prominent art dealer in New York, and he's set my first exhibition in Paris for next month."

"You're going, of course?" Caro sat up straight and clapped. "Paris. That is so-o-o deliciously romantic."

"I knew you could do it. Will you keep your contract with Regency's?" Toby stuffed another cookie in his mouth.

"Yes. I told Stephens I wouldn't renege on that, and besides, who knows how important that may turn out to be?"

"Congratulations, Carrington." Linc extended a hand. "I'd like to see your work sometime."

"Sure. Stop by my studio any time.

"Caro, we never thought we'd have such a famous and rich friend, did we? Man, we should feel privileged you're sitting right here in our unprestigious home." Toby's face beamed.

"Don't be foolish."

Andy had had a haircut and his hair shone in the lamplight. She'd never paid much attention to his square jaw and aristocratic nose. Would never have described them as such, but tonight, he was...there wasn't another word for it.

Handsome. Brown eyes. Modern-styled blond hair. Perfect combination. He looked so happy. So contented.

His gaze flicked to her face. "My first art show is May seven. I'm thinking it will be the making or the breaking of my work. I'd love for you to be there, Caroline. It would mean a lot to me. Will you go as my guest?"

Caro's heart fluttered. Go? To Paris? She'd always dreamed of going on her honeymoon with her imaginary-turned-real prince.

Then her gaze focused once more on Andy's face. With Andy? The boy she'd always despised? The man she didn't want?

But to go to Paris—even if it was with Andy. He was bribing her, but what a bribe. Could she resist? Did she even want to?

She gulped, and her voice croaked when she answered Andy's question. "I'd *love* to go."

Andy's eyes lit with warmth.

But Caro didn't care. She wasn't even going to think about Andy getting his way.

She refocused on her dream. *Paris. The city of love.*

Her glance flicked to Linc.

Chapter Twenty

"I'm off to pick up some groceries." Caro called to her brother early the next morning.

A chuckle reached her ears. "Good, because I don't fancy starving, and if the fridge is any indication—"

Caro peeked into the office. "By the looks of the bulge around your stomach—"

"What?" Toby jumped to his feet and eyed his middle. "I don't have an ounce of fat on my body."

"Just kidding. You're too smug for your own good." She waltzed away, tossing back her last comment.

His grumble followed her out the door.

Caro strolled down the street and gaped at the world in general. Life was good. This past weekend had been a step forward in her relationship with Linc, in spite of his kids' teasing. Last night had been full of sparkling intrigue with Linc. Had he almost kissed her on the front porch?

And Andy's humongous news. She was thrilled he wanted her to go with him to Paris. The most romantic city in the world, wasn't it? Not that she entertained any thoughts in that direction, but what an opportunity and tons of fun thrown into the bargain. If Andy Carrington was foolish enough to spend the money for her trip, then she was agog to go.

Of course, he wouldn't be a shabby escort—just the opposite. She frowned. When had he changed from being an annoyance to *handsome?*

If only Linc could go too.

She thrust her hands deep in her pockets and felt like whistling to let out some of the excitement bubbling inside of her like an underground hot spring.

One of the store windows held a pattern of china she loved, and she paused to study it. The china made her think of food, and her stomach growled in anticipation of the chicken noodles she planned on preparing for supper. Caro hadn't cooked a real meal in ages. Something more than thrown together box meals and sandwiches sounded devastatingly appetizing.

It was some minutes later before the moving reflection on the windowpane caught her attention. What was going on? Whirling, she stared at the red-headed girl who clung to Andy Carrington's arm like she owned him. She beamed up into his smiling face and when he nodded she slid her hand down until her hand clasped his. With swinging arms, they strolled to the crosswalk and waited for the light to change.

Caro stood as if frozen. Her heart, which had sung before, now moaned a funeral dirge. What right did Miss Lauren New York have to come here and try to steal away her friends?

The couple chatted, and once, Caro was sure, Andy glanced her direction. But instead of speaking, he bowed his head and spoke to the girl at his side.

She bit her lip, debating. Should she march ahead and confront them. Make them speak and acknowledge her, or run away as fast as her frozen heart would allow? She blinked several times trying to get the annoying sting from behind her eyes to ease.

Andy and Lauren crossed the street and headed the opposite direction, not looking back. Not looking at anyone. And definitely not seeing her.

Caro turned, too, and headed home. Shopping could wait till the next time rain froze in mid-July. She wasn't hungry anymore.

~*~

The old fashioned bell tinkled when the door opened late that morning. Caro, deep into writing the first scene of the play for the Clarksburg church, looked up.

Arms laden with packages, Toni hurried toward her. "What are you doing?"

"Working on Linc's play. What have you got?"

"Clothes. Time for lunch. Put up your sign and let's go upstairs." Toni headed for the stairs.

Caro stared after her. What on earth? She hurried to lock the front door and ran up the stairs after her friend.

Toni was spreading clothes out everywhere in the tiny room that served as Caro's bedroom. Caro stood in the doorway and gaped. "What is all this?"

Her friend turned to face her, smiling. "You're going with Andy to Mr. Bennett's dinner, aren't you? Then, voila, I'm your fairy godmother today."

"You bought me clothes?"

"Don't worry, you can count it as a loan. I knew you wouldn't have time to go shopping, so I picked up a few different outfits for you. See what you think."

Caro walked over slowly and stared down at the gowns. "Couldn't I wear something I already have? I bought a gown when I went out to dinner with Linc."

"No. That won't suit." The doubtful expression flitting across Toni's face vetoed the idea as if it was the worse one Caro had ever voiced.

"You want to show me what you have suitable for a fancy dinner?"

Well, if Toni refused the one she'd spent two weeks' salary on, then...

The clothes hanging behind her closet door didn't promise any good answers, but Caro marched to her closet and yanked out the first thing she touched. When she met Toni's gaze, she dissolved into giggles. "Okay, thanks, Toni. I guess I should have been thinking about this, but I've been so busy."

"So you said before." Toni helped Caro slide the shimmering pale green dress over her head, and fastened the back of it.

Caro looked in her full-length mirror at herself and caught her breath. "It's beautiful. I love it."

"Don't make any decisions yet. Let's try them all on. Let's see, we've got, besides this green one, the blue, and a gorgeous lilac that will turn your skin to satin."

"Right." Caro lifted her arms so Toni could pull the dress off her. It would take more than a color to satin-ize her skin.

"Why are you so busy now?" Toni shook the blue dress and lifted it.

"I want to get the first couple of scenes in the play I'm writing for Linc done this month. If I can get that much done, then I'll have one more to go. I'm making it a three-act play. That's plenty for a church play. Even if it is televised." Caro gazed at herself in the blue dress. "Oh, dear. I love this one too. Toni, these gowns are positively gorgeous. Where did you get them?"

"Where I get mine for one of Perrin's college dinners. Of course, I don't attend as many important functions as you might be facing in the near future."

"What are you talking about?"

"Andy. With Andy becoming so popular, he's sure to be attending a great many fancy and elite dinners and parties. You'll have to dress to compliment him, dear."

"Me? Who says I'll be the one going to all these dinners? Maybe he'll decide to take Lauren Stephens. After all, he's working with her dad now."

Toni slid a bemused look in her direction. "Who did he want to attend one of Bennett's dinners with him? Who did he think to ask to his first showing? And in Paris, of all places?"

"He just wants someone from home there with him. That's all it is." Toni adjusted the bodice of the lilac dress as she slipped it on and avoided Toni's gaze. "I mean, he could have asked Toby, but you know Toby. He wouldn't want to be away from the shop that long. Not even for his best friend."

Best friend. Andy and Toby were no longer best friends.

Nonsense. That was just words Andy spouted because he wanted to impress her. To convince her to date him.

"Enjoy yourself and leave the rest to God."

"But I want Linc. He's...he's the man of my dreams. Handsome and confident and exciting."

The gaze that met hers in the mirror was sober and thoughtful. "And Andy isn't?

"Y-e-s, he is all that."

"I'm not trying to make your decision for you. Only you can do that. But sometimes dreams change. We just have to remember that when we wake up."

~*~

Caro waited in the shop for Andy to pick her up. She hovered over the computer, trying to think of the next scene in the play, but her brain couldn't get past Toni's words. *Dreams change...*

Was she still asleep? Unable to recognize—no. She wouldn't go there.

Linc with his black hair and tall strong body? Someone new. And different. He excited her. How could this be wrong? Why had God allowed him to enter her life if it wasn't right?

Or Andy—good ol' Andy who she'd known all her life.

The tiny ballerina on the music box beckoned, drawing her, reminding her—again—that her life was going nowhere. She let her fingers find and twist the tiny key in the back. The figure began twirling, around and around, making its way across and back forever dancing to the tinny music pouring from the box. Going nowhere.

Would her life ever stop spinning out of control? She felt like a rope people tugged on to pull the other side across the centerline. She blinked to keep the tears from rolling down her cheeks. Toni had stopped by after the shop closed today and helped her do her hair and get dressed for the dinner. She didn't want to ruin what her friend had pronounced as perfect.

The tapping on the door sent her rushing to it. Andy, in his black tailor-made suit thrust a bouquet of daisies at her.

Her favorites. She touched the white petals, her mind whispering the words she'd chanted as a child. *He loves me. He loves me not.*

Lauren Stephens.

The name blared in her mind, smothering out the outrageous softening toward Andy it'd felt seconds earlier.

"You bought me flowers? Why did you do that?" She bit back the accusation she wanted to spout. *Why buy me flowers when you insist on holding hands with Lauren Stephens right in front of the whole town?*

"I knew you probably wouldn't wear a corsage, but I thought I'd get these for you as a thank you for going with me."

The light in his eyes dimmed, and a sword of sorrow thrust itself into her heart. *Be nice*, as Toby was fond of instructing her.

"They're still your favorites, aren't they?"

"Yes." She'd always felt sorry for them because so many people shunned them, thinking them common. But she liked their pure white petals and sunny middles. Seemed like a winning combination to her. Caro snipped the stems with quick snaps.

"They suit you."

"I wouldn't say that."

"I would." Andy's quiet words penetrated her concentration, and she looked up. When she saw his confident, knowing look fastened on her, the shivers tingled her nerve endings and spread to her fingers causing her to drop the scissors she held.

Choosing one of the vases from a shelf, she filled it with water then set the stems in it, effectively turning her back to Andy. "I wish you wouldn't have gotten them for me. But they're nice, and I love them. Thanks, Andy."

Outside, Andy seated her in his bug and hurried around to his side of the car. With his fingers on the key, he looked over at her, the tenderness in his tone tugging at her emotions. "You are beautiful. I won't have you to myself a minute tonight when the men get a look at you."

"Are you flattering me?" The rush of heat had her interlocking her fingers to keep from fanning herself.

"You deserve to be flattered." He reached over and touched her cheek. "Your eyes are dewy brown. You haven't been crying, have you?"

Yikes. How did he always know what was going on with her? She tossed a question back at him. "Why would I do that?"

He shrugged and didn't answer, but Caro had a weird feeling he knew she'd pushed back the tears before he'd arrived.

The five minute drive was quiet. Two men directed the parking at Bennett's house. After Andy had parked and gone around to help Caro out, he took her elbow as they walked toward the house.

The immense and daunting dwelling seemed to be threatening her to watch her step, and Caro swallowed her anxiousness. "I think I'm a little nervous."

Andy's grip on her elbow tightened, and he laughed. "You'll do fine. Just be yourself and don't try to be anyone else."

"Then what am I doing in this?" Caro looked down at the splendid gown she wore.

"I want you to enjoy yourself."

"Since when did you begin going to such functions?" Caro gulped in several breaths before settling her gaze on his face.

"Since Bennett first asked me." He looked down at her as they walked up the steps. "He seemed to like me, and it gave me a foot in the door for practice. I was so shy at the very first dinner, I barely said five words."

She couldn't imagine Andy like that. He was quiet, true, but he'd never been shy.

"Bennett and I hit it off, and now we see each other occasionally. I have him for lunch now and then. He asks me to attend a few social events. I'm beginning to enjoy it."

This was a new Andy. Someone totally different then her brother's—should she say it?—best friend.

"You will, too." As the door opened, Andy squeezed her hand. "Give yourself a chance. You're beautiful and look like a million bucks."

The laughter bubbled up inside her. She

couldn't help it. "A million, the man says. He thinks I'm cheap. Ha. I'm worth far more than that."

If she lived to be a hundred, she'd never forget the expression that flicked across Andy's face. Shock? Wonder? Astonishment? Assurance? *Rapturous joy?* And then it was gone, and he tucked her hand within his arm. He kept strolling forward, but his gaze stroked her face and his whisper reached only her ears.

"You can just bet you are."

Bennett spotted and came to greet them. He reached for Caro's hand, his manner friendly. "If it isn't the attractive detective. Andy told me he was bringing a friend."

It took a second to pull her own gaze from Andy's, and then she focused on the older man greeting them.

Would it be too rude to ask him if he'd done any spying lately with his binoculars? Instead she plastered on the sweetest she could muster and answered him. "He twisted my arm."

The old man threw back his head and laughed. Several people stared. "Andy, I like this girl of yours. Fresh and unafraid to speak her mind. Come with me, dear, and I'll introduce you around. Andy..."

Andy waved them away. "I'm fine."

Caro looked at Andy over her shoulder as she allowed his neighbor to lead her away. She used her eyes to plead with him to save her. He mouthed one word back at her. *Later.*

It was a full half-hour before they'd finished making the round of the room. Caro felt her mind swimming with names. While Bennett was occupied with a business friend, she slipped away and half-hid behind a gigantic rubber plant to watch the other people in the room. She hadn't seen Andy since Bennett had whisked her away.

A movement across the room caught her eye. Andy stood with a cluster of people, laughing and seemingly enjoying himself. He was talking, gesturing with his hands as he spoke, and all those with him seemed to listen intently.

He looked so at home in this setting.

His blond hair, bleached from his hours in the sun, shone with good health. And he really looked good in that suit. Showed off his wide shoulders and gave his lean body more build.

Obviously the women in the group thought he was attractive the way they eyed him. She ought to march over there and shoo them away. But her attention rested on someone else.

His assistant stood near Andy's group and seemed to be a part, and yet she stood a few feet outside the group, indicating otherwise. Her features revealed no animosity at the others' exclusion.

How could she not feel it?

She couldn't. With deliberate movements Stephanie thrust out a hand and set her glass on a passing waiter's tray, then slipped across the room. She hesitated as if to speak to Bennett, but when he ignored her, moved on and disappeared out the door.

Leaving? Headed to the bathroom? Who knew? But she could sympathize a bit.

After another sip of her fancy-flavored iced tea, she set it down on a nearby table. With a quick glance around, she slipped from the room and went in search of a bathroom. She opened several doors before locating one.

There was no hurry to return to the great room. She'd just wander around amusing herself for awhile. After all, hadn't Bennett said to make herself at home? She certainly needed a break from all that overblown, stale air.

The library was tempting and took up ten minutes of her time. She stuck her head in a couple other rooms but had no idea what function they served. Then on impulse pulled open a door at the end of the hall that was a storage room. She was about to close the door when something caught her attention. Bending over, she tugged at the large flat object wrapped in brown paper to pull it away from the shelves.

One of Andy's stolen paintings?

Caro sat back on her heels and debated with herself. What to do? It could very well be Andy's, but then what if it wasn't? And really, why should it be? But who kept paintings hidden in storage rooms? Probably lots of people, but if it was valuable wouldn't it be in a safe or hanging on a wall? And even if it wasn't, why didn't they have it stored in the attic?

She needed to see the painting. She'd know by just looking at it. Gloomy? Andy's, for sure.

Don't. Her brain screamed.

Do it. Her heart insisted.

With a shrug, she ignored her brain and started to sit on the floor cross-legged, then remembered her dress. With one hand she swiped it across the floor and grimaced at the streaks of dust. Yuk. She didn't want to ruin her fancy dress.

She checked both ways down the hall. With no one in sight, she bent to pick up the package and lugged it to the library where she leaned the painting against the back of the sofa. Pulling a chair close, she went to work.

As hard as she tried to ease it off without ripping it into shreds, the paper wouldn't cooperate. At last she tore into it. She'd have to figure out how to replace the wrapping later. Or confess her doings to Bennett.

Voices penetrated through the heavy door once, and Caro paused, holding her breath. "Go away," she whispered and then held her breath again. "Don't come in here and ask me what I'm doing."

At least until she figured out what Bennett was up to.

When she could no longer hear the voices, she looked at the painting. Andy's. There was no denying the gloominess of this one.

A child walking on a stone fence, arms outstretched for balance. One foot in the air as if the little boy were teetering and on the edge of falling. On the near side a vicious-looking dog stood against the fence, jaws gapping.

Caro shivered. Horrible.

At the bottom, in the right hand corner, scribbled in Andy's nearly unreadable handwriting, was Andy's name.

So. Now she knew.

Nevertheless, the question remained. Why did Bennett have it? *Was* it one of the stolen paintings? Or, he could have bought it. One thing for sure, she needed to get this back into the storage room pronto and then go talk to Andy. She wished she'd asked before now what the stolen paintings looked like.

Shoving the brown paper under the sofa, she bent then to pick up the painting.

And heard voices.

Voices in the hall.

Voices outside the library.

Coming in here?

Her gaze flitted to the curtained French doors. Her mind prodded at her nervous reflex system. *Move.*

A quick glance around, then she grabbed the picture and scurried around the sofa. There was just enough room to squeeze behind it, and she dropped to the floor, allowing the heavy painting to drop to her legs. She winced. Ouch.

She tried to will her body to shrink into the size of a beach ball as she listened to the microscopic sound of a door knob turning, of the clackety-click of shoes on the wood floor, of the voice that spoke even as it drew closer to the sofa.

"Carring...doesn't suspect anything, but that friend of his is nosing around."

Almost a whisper. Was the person trying to disguise his voice or did he not want others to hear what he said? Had he said *Carrington*?

"You called me down here to tell me that?" The second voice boomed angrily around the room.

"Is this working or not? You agreed to be a part of my..., but I get the feeling you're weaseling out. You can't have it two ways. Either we're together or..."

Together? In a scheme? Were they talking about Andy's paintings? What was this person talking about? Who was he?

"I can do better on my own." Booming Voice insisted.

"It's not about the money, you idiot."

"It is for me."

A third voice spoke, but so softly Caro could barely make out any words.

"Shut up, both of you. I agreed...but I like him...not at all like you insisted. I'm tired of your..."

She'd heard that voice...Was it...*Bennett?*

The whispering voice snapping back an answer sent the chilliest chill bumps Caro had ever experienced. "I've never forgotten. How could you?"

Angry Voice must be moving about. Caro hoped he didn't decide to stroll to the French window where he'd have a perfect view of her—that is, if he looked in the right direction.

Whispering Voice went on, almost pleading. "Didn't I tell you it would work? Already, some of the bigger papers are picking up on it."

"So you tell me how to keep the girl out of it."

Yikes. Was the guy talking about her?

"Bribe her. Tell her anything to keep her mouth shut. We don't want him to know yet."

The venom in Whispering Voice words scared Caro, and she wasn't easily frightened.

"And if that doesn't work? She's pretty smart."

Silence.

"Then we'll have to go to Plan B, and I always have a Plan B."

Caroline shivered. Who were these jerks? Should she stand and let them know she was listening to their every word?

"It's time for dinner. I need to get back before I'm missed." Third Voice's quiet words faded.

Footsteps. Two sets. A door opening.

Where was the third set of steps?

"Fools." The whispering voice muttered. "I'll kill them all."

The clackety-click steps headed to the door, and the gentle click of a door shutting echoed across the room.

Caro sucked in a breath of air and collapsed against the back of the sofa. What on earth was going on? And who had they been?

She'd not heard anyone here at this dinner with that super-sonic booming voice. The third voice was familiar—Bennett?—but so low she could barely hear what he was saying. But the whispering one—the venomous one—troubled her, or should she say, scared her? There was a thread of hate running through it that meant trouble for—who? Andy?

Andy, where are you?

Caro edged herself to her knees and peeked over the back of the sofa, saw that the door was firmly closed, and rose. Grabbing the painting, she headed for the hall.

It was time for the meal. Quiet Voice had been afraid he'd be missed.

Now she was wondering if she would be. And who would come looking for her.

Chapter Twenty-one

Crazy idea, yeah. But Andy'd been waiting on this dinner to see if it was as he suspected and hoping it would help bring him and Caroline closer to finding a thief.

Ever since a car had almost run him over, he'd wracked his brain. A car like that wasn't easy to overlook, whether you were into cars or not. And given it was in topnotch shape—he could tell from the sound of the engine and those nighttime street lights reflecting off the shine on the car—well, those were solid reasons to think someone took pride in keeping it in mint condition.

That's what he wanted to find out tonight.

Cause he'd gone over and over all the people he knew in Appleton who even remotely could be considered as someone who'd own a car like that.

He was about to find out.

Andy snuck through the back of the house and out the door. He swiveled, debating which outdoor building would house such a collector item, and nodded to himself when he spied it.

He twisted the walk-in door knob. Yes. Unlocked and easily accessible. Good. He stepped inside and flashed the small flashlight around the building. Three covered vehicles lined the room, and he wasted no time.

He went from one to the other, lifting the

canvas material to study each one. At the third one, the farthest one away, he threw back the cover and sighed with relief.

Black, vintage car.

Suspicion solved.

This car had almost killed him.

~*~

"Dinner is served."

Caro scampered back into the great room as the words from Bennett's butler echoed around the room. She leaned against the wall, nodded at the couple who gave her a bewildered look, and drew in several gulps of air. Her hands shook with excitement, but she clenched them behind her back to steady herself.

Where was Andy? If she could get to him, she'd let him know what she'd heard. What if he was in danger? Fear bled from her pores. Maybe she should speak with Bennett? Where was *he*?

She stood on tiptoe and scanned the moving clusters of people headed toward the dining room. There.

"Excuse me." She edged around a tall, bald man.

"So sorry." She murmured at two couples as she squirmed between them, then swooped down on Bennett. Beside him stood a successful looking woman, her be-ringed fingers touching his arm.

"Mr. Bennett, I need to talk with you. Now."

The white-haired gentleman stopped his exposition on business in general. "Caroline? What's wrong?"

The woman with Bennett stared at Caro, displeasure written across her forehead. Then with a grimace the lady flounced away.

"I heard something..."

A row of lines appeared on Bennett's forehead. "Caroline, my dear. Are you investigating while at one of my dinners? Please forget your work and enjoy yourself. Now, if you'll excuse me...?"

"But—" Caro stood where she was and watched him go, leading his guests to what she was sure was a superb meal.

And where had Andy gone?

~*~

It was a full two hours later before the dinner finally broke up.

Caro had never been so glad to see Andy appear beside her. She leaned in close. "Where have you been? Let's get out of here."

In spite of Andy's confused glance, Caro tugged at his arm, trying to hurry him. He took his time thanking Bennett. Bennett clasped his hand and beamed at him.

"Carrington, we need to get together next week."

And then they were out the door. But just before the big door slammed shut behind them, Caro glanced back, but it wasn't Bennett or any of the guests who caused her to pause.

At the end of the hallway, a tall, dark-haired someone, in a suit as elaborately handsome as any she'd seen tonight, was stepping out the far door.

Was that *Linc*?

There was no more time to recognize the person. Others behind them gave them a subtle push to move on, and Andy took her arm, guiding her toward his blue bug.

As they followed the cars from the parking lot, Andy spoke. "What was your hurry? Is something wrong?"

"I've been trying to tell you. Where did you go all evening? I hardly saw you until we sat down at the table and then I had to sit between two guys who kept talking to each other over my head."

"Poor Caroline. I thought you'd enjoy yourself. Bennett's dinners are usually fun. But I'll have to admit tonight was a little...boring. And I looked for you twice but both times you were gone."

"It wasn't boring for me." Caro felt the scene in the library punch her in the stomach again.

"So you did have fun."

"Not fun, but it definitely wasn't boring. At least part of it wasn't."

Andy pressed on the brake pedal to stop at a red light. "What happened?"

"I overheard three people talking."

Andy sent her a pretend-shocked look as he grinned at her. "You weren't eaves-dropping, were you? There are a lot of business matters discussed quietly and settled satisfactorily at his functions."

"You won't think it's so funny when I tell you what I heard."

"Then spit it out. I can't wait any longer."

Was that a smirk coloring Andy's voice "I slipped out of the great room and wandered around a little..."

When she'd finished, there was a moment of silence as he pulled up in front of Undiscovered Treasures. Then he laughed.

"You think it's funny?" The dark street

outside his car window emphasized her foreboding. “Okay. Tell me this. Did you paint a scene of a little boy walking on a wall with a horribly mean-looking dog below him?”

“That was the last one stolen.”

“And I’ve never seen it, so how could I know what it was?”

“And you're sure this painting was in one of Bennett’s closets?”

“Storage room. Wrapped in brown paper and shoved back against some shelves.”

“I don’t believe it.”

His words took the breath from her. He’d never, never doubted anything she’d said before. Did he doubt her now? “You don’t believe me?”

“I should have said: I can’t believe Bennett would steal from me. It doesn’t make sense. There has to be something you’re missing here.” Andy's head was moving back and forth.

Anger at Andy’s choice of words suddenly raced through her veins. “Me? Why does it have to be me who’s missing something? Why does it have to be me who does all the detective work? I’m the one who has all the suggestions. I’m the one who finds all the clues. And I’m the one who I guess, should find your paintings, is that it?”

Her voice had risen. She could feel her hands shaking again.

“Caroline. I didn’t mean that. I really appreciate...”

“My name is Caro. You appreciate me so much you don’t believe what I’m telling you. Well, I’m repeating myself again by telling you there’s more to your wonderful neighbor than you realize. It very well could have been him hatching some plot against you. Did you hear him flattering the woman-shark who sat beside him at the table?"

"No. But they are old business buddies. Always buttering each other up to get the best of the deal."

"What kind of business buddy? What does she do?"

"I don't know for sure." Andy's forehead wrinkled in concentration. "I think maybe she's in sales, and not the average salesperson type of thing. Valuable objects, art—"

He broke off and stared at her.

"Let me just list why I think there's more going on. First, he was spying on you the day the newspaper people came."

His attempt to interrupt didn't work. Caro waved at him and went ahead talking.

"Don't interrupt me. Then he ignored—refused to answer questions that should have been simple to answer." She sniffed.

"He's a private man."

"You keep saying that. Why is he? It makes me wonder about him even more. And tonight, I find a stolen painting in his house. He probably has the other ones hidden somewhere too, just waiting till you get famous, then he'll sell them underground and make a killing off your hard work."

"Stop. Bennett is rich. I mean, way rich. Far richer than I'll ever be, or even care to be."

"Some people feel they can never have too much money."

"Not Bennett."

Caro flounced in her seat, rocking the tiny

car. "Why are you defending this guy? What's he to you?"

Andy's voice was low, quiet, with a thread of something running through it. "He's my friend."

"You never said you were that close to him."

"We're not. But can you understand that I mentally place him in the position of the father and the grandfather I lost too soon? Bennett doesn't know I look at him that way."

"You think he cares about you? Then why does he have your missing painting in his house? Just tell me that."

"I don't know. And, really, I don't care. Whatever the reason is, I'm sure I'll find out. Soon enough."

"I want—no, I need to know now. I won't sit calmly by until Mr. Rich Guy decides to explain his actions. I think he's taking advantage of you. I'm going to call the cops."

"No. Absolutely not."

"No? What do you mean?"

"I mean I won't call the cops on Bennett. And I can't allow you to either."

"He has something on you?" Caro whispered the words, sudden fright for Andy climbing her back with steely claws.

"Of course not." Andy threw his arm over the back of her seat. "Caroline, I want you to forget this investigation. Let's drop it. You've done enough."

"You want me to quit? Forget it? After the time I spent on this for you?" Truth be told, she'd done little, what with getting to know Linc. "Something is wrong with Bennett. I feel it, and I wish you'd believe me."

The distant form in Bennett's house, striding away from the departing guests, blazed in her mind. *Had* it been Linc?

"I'm not sure. I prefer you forget it for now. I appreciate..."

The anger that had moved sluggishly before now stirred deep inside her being like a slowly awakening volcano after a decade of sleep. She was jerked back to her growing up years—to the years when Toby and Andy had ignored and laughed at her ideas and thoughts.

Her lips formed the words even as her brain clutched at them, trying to stuff them back into the basket of her mind. But, as if they had a mind of their own, they refused to be stuffed, spewing forth like red-hot lava.

"Andy Carrington. I'm angrier with you than I've ever been. You've always been passive and too laid back for your own good. Spineless with a yellow stripe running straight up that back of yours. Well, let me tell you, I thought you were changing in the last few weeks, but you haven't, not one iota. You're still the same weak wimp I've known forever—for...for way too long."

Caro gripped the door handle, desolation like a thundercloud hovering over her. She'd done it now. Might as well finish the destruction. "And you kissed me. Don't ever do it again. In fact, I don't ever want to see you again."

With a jerk, she squeezed the handle until it unlatched, and shoved at the door with her shoulder. With another look at Andy's ghost-like face, she jumped from the car.

"I was going to say thanks for the evening,

but I won't lie. I'm not thankful for it, and I won't say it." She started to slam the door and stopped. "I'll see myself in."

She did slam it then and stomped toward her business and home. Caro didn't look back when she heard the engine start and chug down the street. But she rested her head on her front door and groaned. Was that a rumble she heard? Or a snore from a volcano that'd done too much damage and was now settling down for another long sleep?

~*~

Caro stooped to pick up the lilac gown she'd flung into a corner of her bedroom a week ago. Hanging the dress carefully on its hanger, she jerked the plastic covering over it and tossed it on a chair. She'd drop it off at the shelter. Who on earth would want it, she didn't know, but she couldn't bear to look at the thing again.

Caro sighed. It'd been such a beautiful gown.

"Want me to get rid of that for you?" Toni lifted the plastic wrapped gown and slid the hanger hook over Caro's door.

"Would you? I can't...won't wear the gown again. Ever." She tilted her head to look at her friend, but Toni didn't speak.

Wasn't she even curious what Caro was talking about?

"Linc's picking you up at six?" At Caro's nod, Toni went on. "Then we'll meet you at the Charleston dinner theatre about six-thirty."

"Who all decided to go?" Would Andy be there? Caro's stone heart lurched at the thought of seeing him, of trying to stay away from him, of ignoring him.

Toni shrugged. "I don't know. You need to ask Linc. He's the one who did the inviting and worked out the details. Quite a few are going, from what I heard. Some from his church and ours."

"Are you sure the pink dress is the one I should wear?" Caro peered anxiously at her friend. "I want to look really nice for Linc."

"You'll wow him tonight." Toni stepped up beside Caro and hugged her. Her grip tightened, loosened, then she headed for the door. "I'm praying for you. God knows what he's doing."

Yeah, but do I? Caro's gaze followed Toni.

~*~

Six-twenty-nine. Linc's knock came right on time, and Caro's heart leaped at the sound. She hurried to answer the door.

He held out a box to her. "This is for you."

"Thanks. Come on in a minute." Caro motioned him in.

"For just a second. We're right on time. Don't want to be late, do we? Have you seen Midsummer's Night Dream?"

The pink and white orchid corsage was exquisite and warmed her hurting heart as she pinned it to her shoulder. So why did her glance linger on the wilting daisies Andy had given her? "It's beautiful. Thank you. I feel like a princess."

Linc took her hand and linked his fingers through hers. "You are to me."

For an instant, Caro wondered if Linc would kiss her tonight, and would she feel a tingle on her lips as she had when Andy...

No. She would not think of him. She was

way too angry.

"I owe you an explanation." He offered once they were in the car and on their way.

"You do?"

"I want you to know I'm uncomfortable talking about this, but because I feel you need to understand, I'm going to do it." Linc sighed but still stared through the front window of his SUV. "DeeDee Reynolds."

"Oh, her." The woman's beautiful features mocked her memory.

"For a long time after my wife died, I wasn't interested in socializing any. Then gradually I started dating, but nothing serious. An occasional dinner, an event that demanded a partner, things like that. When DeeDee caught my attention, I realized what an attractive woman she was. One I'd seen many times and knew as an acquaintance from our church family."

Caro shifted in her seat so she'd have a better view of her date.

"I grew to like DeeDee. She's confident in her abilities and intellectual."

When Linc hesitated for so long, Caro prompted him, "Then?"

"Then just when I thought we were ready to get more serious, things changed."

"How do you mean?"

Linc shrugged, and Caro realized he was embarrassed. "Little things. She became clingy. She threw several tantrums over obligations I had with the children. Said they were spoiled and despicable. Her sister called two times to chew me out because of so-called slights I'd given DeeDee."

"Did you, Linc?"

"No, I didn't, Caro. I'm not that type of person, and I believe in practicing my faith."

His answer was so straight forward, how could she not... "I believe you."

"The crisis came when she imperiously demanded I send the kids away to live with my parents. That she was in no way interested in raising another woman's kids."

"You're kidding."

"I'm afraid not. I know my twins can be outrageous at times."

"You've got that right." Caro burst out laughing. "But I like them."

"Me, too. And I probably do spoil them, but they are my responsibility, not my parents. Just because I don't happen to have their mother to help doesn't lessen my duty to them."

"Do you mind if I ask you one more thing?" She slowly pulled out the list of names she'd found in his SUV.

"What's that?"

At least his voice sounded calm.

"Could you explain what this is? It looks similar to another list I found..."

"Let me see." He reached for it and glanced down. "Where did you say you found this?"

"On the floorboard of this vehicle. It was crumpled, and I thought..."

"What?"

"It might be important, you know, to find the paintings."

"You suspected *me*?"

"No..."

He laughed. "I didn't steal Andy's paintings,

Caro. But, once again I'm going to have to ask you to trust me. I can't explain, right now anyway."

Had she ever had a real occasion to doubt his sincerity? No. Looked like she had no choice but to trust him. "Yeah, I can do that."

He squeezed her hand, and she knew he was pleased.

The silence grew between them, but it wasn't uncomfortable.

Warmth melted through her. He'd not one time given her cause to be angry. Not like Andy with his outrageous opinions. "Thanks, Linc, for sharing with me."

"I'm thinking—"

The sentence didn't get finished. Caro drew in a long breath, the shivers running up her backbone. She knew what he'd been about to say, but was she ready for it?

As Linc changed lanes, she glanced at him. "Who all will be in the group?"

"Here. Take a look." Linc pulled out a paper from his inside coat pocket.

Caro slid her glance down the list. No mention of Lauren Stephens. Or of Andy.

Why wasn't Andy going? Surely Linc had gotten the names of those interested earlier—way before Andy's and her falling out last night, for sure. She'd supposed he'd ask Lauren to be his date.

Not her, of course.

Caro shifted in her seat, the seatbelt tightening. She pulled at it.

"Are you all right? Refasten your belt if it's too tight." Linc steered the big vehicle around a slower moving car.

"Are you sure no one else is coming?"

Linc withdrew his hand. "Who do you mean?"

"I was just wondering." Careful. She didn't want to ruin tonight. *Watch your tongue, girl.*

"There are about twenty-six of us as a group. I was able to reserve a section for us."

"I hope Toni and Perrin can sit at our table."

"I've worked out the seating arrangements. Can't remember where I placed Toni and Perrin, but a couple of my best friends will be at our table."

His gaze rested on her, and she did her best to give him a happy smile. "What's their names?"

"Tamra and Forrest Cooper. He's the head of Cooper Investigations. She runs her own clothing business."

Great. Geniuses.

She wanted her own friends around her tonight. People she could use for comfort, to help her forget.

"I know, Caro. You like to be with your friends." Linc's voice lowered and soothed her nerves as he spoke. He drew in a long breath, hesitated, then continued. "I gave this a lot of thought. I've been with and met your friends for a couple of months. Now it's time you gave mine a chance. I want you to know more of them."

He captured her hand yet again and brought it to his lips. "Most of all, I want them to know you. Know this wonderful woman I've met." He stopped and a peculiar look bled across his face.

What had the ripple of expression across

Linc's face been about? What had he been about to say? That he was beginning to care for her?

That he loved her?

Caro swiveled to stare out the front glass again and was glad to see they'd arrived. The place was impressive, the white stone walls and elegant tall columns giving it a Roman flare.

Linc pulled in front of the classy-looking building, and an attendant hustled to meet him. Linc took her arm. "Come with me. Let's check out the cherub fountain. They say those who toss coins into the fountain at the same time will forever..."

He looked down at her, turned her so she faced him, and gripped her forearms.

"What, Linc?" Caro looked up at this dark handsome man she cared so much about.

"They fall in love with each other. Of course, that's local legend."

What fun. "Why haven't I heard about this?"

"Maybe because you've never before been here with the man you were supposed to fall in love with."

Linc? What are you saying? Caro had no idea if she'd spoken aloud or not. Her mind whirled with his inference.

"Maybe me."

It wasn't a question, but a statement. A definite statement of conviction.

Linc let go of her and dug in his pockets, pulled out a penny and tossed the single cent up in the air then catching it. "I can't believe I have only one measly penny on me."

"Maybe we can throw it in together."

"No, I don't think so. We've got to each have one."

"I probably have one. Hold on." Caro opened the minuscule bag she carried. Her fingers touched the change in the bottom and pulled out a copper coin. "Got it. Are we ready?"

"Okay. I'll count to three and we'll toss. Ready? One, two, three."

They tossed their coins, and both laughed as they walked close together toward the entrance.

As Linc opened the door for her, he spoke. "You're fun to be with. You bring out the nonsense in me."

Caro paused and cocked an eyebrow at him. "Don't we all hold a little of that inside us? Some just let it out better."

"Linc. Hey, Linc." Linc turned toward the voice.

The couple hurrying toward the man beside her captured his attention. But she glanced back toward the cherub fountain, her heart racing like a souped-up car. Was love in the air for Linc and herself?

Had she made a big mistake tossing it outside the fountain?

Chapter Twenty-two

Toni and Perrin sat at the next table. When Caro returned from filling her plate at the buffet, she paused beside Toni and leaned down to whisper. “Where’s Andy? I thought he was coming?”

“No. I called his cell phone, and he said he wouldn’t be coming.”

Caro’s heart settled somewhere in the pit of her stomach. “Do you suppose he’s busy with Stephens?”

“Maybe. Doesn’t Toby know?”

“I haven’t asked him.”

“Hi, Linc. Taking good care of our friend here?” Toni glanced at the man who stepped up beside Caro.

He slipped an arm around Caro’s shoulder and pulled her against him with an affectionate hug. “The best. By the way, our church’s production runs through the rest of the summer. Why don’t you two run over and see it? I’m sure you’ll enjoy it. The cast does a tremendous job.”

Toni and Perrin exchanged glances. “We might just do that.”

“Great. Let me know when, and I’ll reserve front seats for you. Let me take that for you.” Linc took Caro’s plate and set it at her place, then waited to help her sit.

Caro turned back to her friends. “I’ll talk to

you guys later. Come by the shop soon, Toni?"

When Toni nodded, Caro moved away. As Linc sat down beside her, he leaned close and whispered. "Your friend Andy said when I called him, he wouldn't be able to come tonight as he had plans to be out of town."

"I see."

And she did see more than Linc realized. Andy had left town. She wondered if Toby had known Andy was gone. Of course, he had his upcoming opening art exhibit soon. Had he gone to New York again? Was West Virginia too small for him now?

Her lip stung where she bit it, but she ignored it and shoved the slice of roast beef on her plate closer to the suddenly unappetizing asparagus. It was her fault. She'd been the one to get angry over his refusal to see who had his paintings. Right now, cooled down, she had to admit her anger seemed petty. She was the one who'd been nasty, calling him wimpy and weak. She was the one who'd said she never wanted to see him again.

And he'd taken her at her word.

She became aware that Linc had obviously said something funny because everyone was laughing but her. When he looked at her, she mumbled. "Sorry, I was thinking."

Linc lowered his voice. "About...?"

"Nothing important." Really? Her heart had tumbled back up to her chest, a heavy piece of granite belying her words.

His gaze lingered on her longer than was comfortable, but Caro forked a piece of beef, shoved it into her mouth and avoided his look.

Minutes later, she still struggled to swallow

it. Stomach heaving, Caro jumped to her feet. As she passed the table, she threw Toni a beseeching look, ran for the restroom, and dropped to her knees in one of the stalls. Toni, on her heels, thrust a wet paper towel in her hand. Her friend's cool fingers gently rubbed the back of her neck, and Caro relaxed. She struggled to her feet, her chest heaving, her hands trembling.

"Thanks. I don't know what's the matter with me." She wobbled to the sink and rinsed her mouth.

The long breath of air Toni drew in precluded what Caro knew would be some advice. Loving and sincere, but probably not what she wanted to hear. Or did she?

"Come over here and sit on this bench. I think you'd better tell me what's going on."

Caro sank against the back of the bench. Closing her eyes, she mumbled, "Do I have to?"

She couldn't see her, but heard the smile in Toni's voice when she answered. "Yes, you do. What are friends for?"

"Okay. I told Andy he was a wimp, and I never wanted to see him again."

Silence.

Caro stood it as long as she could, then opened one eye.

Toni's downcast expression didn't only look gloomy, it reeked of bleakness. Uh, oh.

"I'm sure you had a good reason for telling him those end-of-the-world statements? I know you didn't do it just because you were angry?" Toni sent a hopeful glance her way.

She hid her face in her hands, the better to not see Toni's disappointment. "I *was* angry at him."

More silence. Sighs. Not one, but two. Oh, dear. She was trying gentle Toni's patience.

"Well, here's what happened..." By the time, Caro was done, tears were streaming down her face. And although Toni didn't cry, her lashes were wet.

She shook her head for the longest minute in Caro's life, then leaned forward and pulled Caro to her, murmuring in her ear. "Dear, dear, Caro. You are the best—and the worst—friend I've ever had. What are we going to do with you?"

"Saw me asunder? Hire a hit man to do away with me? Burn me at the stake?" Caro whispered the words.

Toni laughed and thrust Caro away from her. "That's why I love you so much. You never hold a grudge for long, and you've always been ready to admit it when you've done wrong."

If only that was true. She patted her face with a napkin. "Well, most of the time. I wish I hadn't said those things. If Andy doesn't care if Bennett stole his paints, then why should I? I should have let it rest, but as usual I had to try to prove my point."

"You do know you're going to have to apologize to Andy? He's too precious to all of us to let this rift between you two continue."

"I know. I know." Caro groaned. "How do I get myself into these messes?"

"I don't know." Toni stood. "I honestly don't know."

"We can't all be perfect like you."

"Yeah, right. But maybe I do know why these messes follow you around. Perhaps you act before you pray."

"You're probably right. I know I'm going to have to have a long talk with my heavenly father. A prayer I've been avoiding."

"We'd better get back before Linc and Perrin think we've flown the coop. How are you and Linc doing?"

"I think we're just about ready to take another step." Caro opened the restroom door and spoke thoughtfully.

"Is that what you want?"

"It's what I thought I wanted." Caro voiced the thought that had nibbled at her mind all evening. Was it what she wanted? What God wanted for her?

Had she been so determined to have her dream prince riding up that she'd ignored God's will for her?

~*~

Andy strolled the streets of New York City. Tonight he was meeting with Stephens and some of his important friends for dinner. Today, though, was his.

The city was a far cry from small town Appleton. He missed it, even after being away only a couple of weeks, and wished he was back there.

The thought brought him straight up. He stuck a peppermint in his mouth and leaned against a building.

Had he been wrong to leave Appleton without at least attempting to mend fences with Caroline?

On one of Toby's nightly phone calls, he'd inserted his opinions about his sister. "I can tell she's unhappy. She's such a conscientious

Christian she won't regain that spontaneity of hers until she makes things right with you."

"I don't care whether she apologizes or not. I should let her know what I've found out."

"Andy, you know Caro as well as I do. If you're serious about her, you're going to have to stay firm. You've always been at her beck and call. Now it's time to change your tune."

And he had held strong, trying to leave it in God's hands. It was her move. Hers and God's.

People swarmed around and past him, hurrying, talking on cell phones, and lifting hands to halt taxis. Their voices blended into a dull roar.

Andy lifted his gaze to the bit of sky he could see between skyscrapers. *God, I ask you to give Caroline the strength to do the right thing. I'm sorry I doubted. I know she's the one for me. Send her to me, Lord. Send her to me quickly.*

~*~

The nail bent again. Caro huffed out her impatience. You'd think after five times, she could pound one simple little nail into a wall.

She yanked the nail out and tossed it into a can. Time for coffee.

The old-fashioned doorbell tinkled as she poured a cup of her favorite rich brew.

Linc, his dark hair shining, walked in. "How's my best girl doing?"

"Frustrated right now." Caro indicated the coffeepot. "Want some?"

"Sure." He strode over to the ballerina music box and twisted the key, setting the little figure free from her frozen position. "What's frustrating you? Anything I can do to help?"

"Can you pound a nail?" Caro arched a brow in mock-doubt.

"Well..." He picked up the hammer she'd dropped to the floor and laid it on the countertop. "Where do you want it?"

"I thought you wouldn't be around till next week? Not that I'm complaining."

"Took the day off. Wanted to see you again."

"That sounds promising." Caro eyed him. "Or is it dire news?"

He lifted the hammer again, then followed her to where she'd poked several holes in the wall with her own attempts.

"Here. I don't know what kind of hard wood is behind this drywall. Surely not oak." She turned.

Linc stood right behind her, his face inches from her own.

Caro heard as from a distance the tinny music flowing out of the music box and felt her throat go dry. "Linc?"

His lips tipped up. His gaze roved over her face. His husky voice was so low if hundreds of ears had been listening, they wouldn't have heard one inflection. "Caro. I think I'm falling for you."

He's such a gorgeous guy. Caro sighed.

His high-watt smile dimmed. "Is that depressing?"

Caro whispered her words, her heart rate erratic, afraid of saying the wrong things. "No. It's...it's very wonderful, Linc. I feel like the luckiest girl alive."

And...the saddest.

Linc's head tilted. "Do I hear a 'but'?"

Ducking under his arm to avoid that

searching look, she moved to one of the stools and sat, patting the one next to hers.

For a moment Linc didn't join her, and then he settled on the stool beside her. He leaned on the counter with his forearms, but for another long moment he didn't speak. Tapping his fingers together, he waited.

"I think..."

"I want..."

They laughed then.

"You first." Linc offered, spreading his hands in an expansive move.

"No, you go first." Caro's heart blanched at the thought of saying what was on her heart first.

"You know you've become very precious to me. I think, I believe I... we could have God's approval on this." Linc's sigh echoed her own. "But..."

Why? Why couldn't her heart behave and do what it was told to do?

"You would fit right into my church. Those who've met you love you and everyone admires your talent. I came here today to talk to you because..."

He let his words hang.

Oh, dear. Oh, dear.

"I'm getting continual vibes you're still thinking a lot about Andy Carrington. I know you say he's just a friend. But is he more than that? Do I have a place in your heart, Caro? Or does your Andy fill the whole space?"

His words were what she'd wanted to hear. He cared and would care more—perhaps even give her his heart—if she just said the word. If she'd just assure him once again Andy really, truly was only a friend.

"I believe I could make you love me."

"I do care for you, Linc." She turned her head away. He didn't need to see the hesitation in her.

"There's that but again." His forefinger touched her chin and turned her face to him. "Can you tell me what I want to hear?"

Could she? With a clear heart? Did she really want to pass up this chance? Give up this wonderful man?

"I...I..."

He rested his arms on the countertop again, his fingers tapping what sounded like a funeral dirge. "You've been giving me hints all along where your heart really is, but I didn't want to listen. I thought I could win your love if I held on."

His words were like the steady drip of rain. Sure and cool. "I was actually glad when I learned Andy had left town. I should have remembered the old adage. Absence makes the heart grow fonder. And though I'm positive you didn't think I'd see, I saw you toss the penny outside the water. On purpose, wasn't it? I was puzzled at first, thinking you really were attracted to me. After praying about it, I knew the answer. It might be a fun activity, but you couldn't do it. It was too untrue for your heart."

Could her face get any redder? Could her guilt feel any worse? She had to be giving her guardian angel a heart attack.

He sat still for a long moment, then his broad shoulders straightened. He tipped his chin in the direction of the winding-down music box. "If you ever decide to get rid of that, let me know. Mother would love it."

Linc stood, and tears stung Caro's eyes. How could she be so stupid as to let him go? She jumped to her feet.

"I...don't..."

"I know, Caro." Linc leaned forward and kissed the tip of her nose. His hands gripped her arms. He lifted her hand and kissed it. "Take care. I'll see you around. I'm sure the church will want more plays."

He turned to leave, but Caro clasped his arm. "Wait. Were you at Bennett's latest party a month ago? I thought I saw—"

"I hoped no one saw me, but I should have known those sharp eyes of yours would."

"You were."

"Yes. But don't ask any more details, Caroline. I can't tell you right now." He chucked her again on the chin. "Someday. Maybe."

"But I have so many questions."

"I know you do and wish I could explain, but I can't. Suffice it for me to tell you: I haven't told you everything about me." He held up a hand when her mouth opened to ask another question. "Nothing I'm ashamed of, but something I'm not at all at liberty to tell. Not even to you. Yet."

"Linc?" Caro edged a step closer to the person who'd been the man of her dreams. "I do wish this had turned out differently for us."

"I know you do." He was so quiet, so still for a moment as if waiting for a miracle to happen.

Checking to make sure her answer was final?

"But we've got to do what our hearts demand, don't we?"

His face was a little sad, and she almost called him back when he headed toward the door.

But she couldn't.

The door banged, and the man she'd thought of as her prince was gone.

Chapter Twenty-three

Caro peeked into Toby's office for the third time. Opened her mouth. Shut it. Opened it. Croaked and coughed.

Toby spoke without turning. His fingers tapped on the keyboard furiously. "What do you need, Caro? I'm busy."

"Sorry."

She moved away from the door but hadn't gone six steps when Toby grabbed her arm.

"Sorry, Sis. Is something wrong?"

Arms crossed, Caro shifted from one foot to the other. "No."

"Time for a break anyway." He stretched. "We got any coffee ready?"

"Sure, I'll get you some."

"I'll get it. Did you eat all the homemade cookies Toni sent over?"

"No." Caro snorted. "You did."

With one hand he carried his cup and linked arms with her to lead her to the counter. "Sit. What have you been up to?"

"Nothing much. Working in the store. Toni and I went shopping one day."

"Did you guys have a good time at the theatre dinner?"

"It was fun."

"You did go with Linc?" Toby eyed her.

"Of course. He's a wonderful man."

"I haven't seen him around for the last two

weeks. Is he that busy?"

Heat burned her cheeks. She was turning into a regular blushing maiden. Toby was nosier than an old woman. She scowled at him. "Quit asking so many questions."

"Okay. Okay." He held up a hand. "You talk then."

Caro searched her mind for something to ask. The only thing looming as big as a semi was the one thing she didn't want to bring up. Yet. "How are you and Amy doing? Still together?"

"Yes. I like her. She's a lot of fun."

"But is she the one?"

"Who knows?" Toby grinned like a Siamese cat who'd stolen the best cream in the house.

"You're not planning on any trips in the near future, are you?"

"Nope."

Was he being dense on purpose? Why couldn't he expand on her questions? He usually never shut up.

"Uh, let's see, what else can I ask you?"

Toby sipped his coffee and set the cup down carefully. "All right. What's going on? You've got something in that pea brain of yours. What do you want?"

Caro twisted on her seat. Laced her fingers together then flattened them on the countertop. Swung her crossed leg. Stopped. Her breath escaped in a huff. Her words came out in a rush. "How's Andy doing?"

"He's fine. Busy." Toby wrapped his hands around his cup. "Having a great time from what he says."

"He's been gone forever." Caro hoped she

hadn't wailed the words.

"A month. He says Stephens is keeping him busy. Meeting prospective clients. Lots of advertising."

"Sounds busy." Why didn't he just come home?

"He is. He's thinking of renting an apartment in New York. Closer and all that stuff."

Had her heart literally stopped beating? "Is he in Paris yet?"

"He flew there the first of the week. His show is in two days."

Silence. Long. Uncomfortable.

"Uh, I...miss him."

Toby turned his head then and looked at her. "You miss him?"

Don't give me a hassle. Just answer the questions and make this easy for me.

"Of course, I do. He's your friend after all, and we've known him forever. I'm not that hard-hearted. Of course, I...I...c-are." Silly tears wet her lashes, and she swiped them away with a gruff wipe. What a crybaby she was.

"I know you do, Sis." Toby's face softened. "What took you so long to admit it? And more important, what are you going to do about it?"

"Do?"

"Are you going to let him get away? I know a very pretty, very young red-head who would like to get her hands on him."

"What can I do?" Caro lifted her hands. "In case you've forgotten, he's across the ocean in a big sophisticated city."

"Go to him."

Caro, whirling around on her bar stool, came to an abrupt stop. "What did you say?"

"I said, go to him. If you're serious and done wishing for the moon when the sun is right above you."

"How? I mean, I can't just walk out and leave you here to run the store by yourself..."

"Of course, you can. When have you ever taken an extensive holiday?"

"There are too many things to do. I'd never get ready in time to be there for his show. I'd need airplane tickets and a passport and clothes, and I don't know what else."

"Amy's already agreed to help out while you're gone. Toni's been shopping for days for you and is due here in about an hour to help you pack. And..." Toby reached inside his pocket and pulled out an envelope. "Open it."

Caro took the proffered envelope, lifted the flap, and stared at the airplane tickets inside. "What? Where did you get these?"

Toby's wide grin beamed at her. "I bought them two weeks ago. I hoped you'd come around. Toni and I've been busy plotting this for days. We thought we'd go crazy waiting on you to make up your mind."

"You knew I'd..."

"Not exactly, but I had a pretty good idea of how my kid sister works. And I prayed God would help you." He raised his hands, let them drop. "This morning is the deadline. After that Toni and I were going to gang up on you."

Her mind whirled in dizzying circles. She couldn't believe this was happening. If anything, she'd hoped to talk to Andy on the phone—if he would talk to her—and make her apologies. But this—this was beyond anything she could have dreamed about.

She slid off her stool and looked at her beloved brother. "Does Andy know about this?"

"Nope. From here on out, it's up to you."

"What if he doesn't want me there? Are you sure I should be flying around the world for something that might turn into a fiasco? What if he decides cute red-heads are right down his alley? That—that Lauren really is who he wants."

"Have I ever steered you wrong?"

"Just a time or two." Caro ducked the mock-punch he aimed at her.

~*~

Clouds, thick and heavy hung around the airplane Caro sat within. She couldn't see a thing. She sighed and picked up a magazine, flipped through it then tucked it back in the pocket of the seat in front of her. She couldn't concentrate on anything but the coming meeting with Andy.

Fear that he would disdain her apology—even though her mind argued otherwise—ate at her. What if the damage she'd shoveled out was too vast? Too, too much for Andy to overlook like he'd done so many times in the past? How could she have ever been so hateful? She groaned, and the man sitting beside her gave her a questioning look.

"Are you all right?" The French accent broke into her concentration.

Leave me alone. I deserve to suffer alone. Still, some reassuring words would be nice.

"I'm flying after a man."

Her airplane companion hmm—hawed

through his white mustache. "Is that so? Many times that is the only way to get what one wants, is it not?"

"I'm afraid I won't be getting what I want."

The smile vanished. "Oui. That kind of meeting."

"I hurt the man very badly, and I'm hoping to apologize. Make amends. Patch things up." Caro stopped her rambling. "If he'll listen to me."

"He will listen. Who could help but listen to such a charming young woman?"

"Thanks. But I'm not at all like that." Why deny the truth?

She must have stumped even his seemingly good will for the man remained silent. Only when they'd buckled up for the plane's landing did he speak again.

"You have room reservations?"

Caro tapped her purse. "My brother and friend took care of everything."

"Would you like a ride? My name is Larmore Merle. My business associates in the United States call me Larry."

Should she? Caro shifted in her seat to eye him. "I don't know you."

"Of course you don't. But I'll be glad to give you some references. I'm well-known here in Paris."

"Okay. I'll make some calls and let you know when we're on the ground."

~*~

Andy tugged at his bow tie again. He needed to forget what could have been and concentrate on this evening. This was important to him, and though Caroline wasn't here to share it with him, he couldn't let that fact destroy this opportunity. God was faithful. He would take care of Caroline.

In spite of the sermon to himself, his spirits insisted on dragging the ground, as Caroline was apt to say. His emotions shrank from thinking of Caroline with Lincoln Tillis. He should have gone to her instead of waiting on her to apologize. He should have insisted on having their rift dissolved. He knew how stubborn she could be. Besides, what did Toby know?

He turned away from the mirror, sick of trying to figure it out. His cell phone rang, and Andy stared at it, counting the rings. As much as he cared about Lauren, he wasn't in any mood to deal with her right now. She'd have to wait. He needed some time alone with his God.

When the phone ceased its ringing, he picked up his Bible, settled in the brocaded chair, and flipped through till he reached his favorite scripture in Psalms 91. Then taking in a deep breath he began reading.

~*~

Caro followed Larry down the ramp of the plane. He stood to one side while she called the references he'd provided. A call to the local police station verified his good reputation, and she turned back to him.

"Satisfied?"

"Yes. But I can't figure out why you're so concerned with me." Caro strode beside the man as he headed to pick up their baggage.

"I'm a minister and asked God this morning to let me meet someone today that needed my help." Mischief twinkled in his eyes. "And, to be totally honest, your pastor contacted a mutual friend who contacted me to watch for you."

"Really?" Caro gulped. Her whole church must have been involved in getting her here.

"Really. When do you meet this man of yours?"

Hers? Hardly. "Tonight at the Art De Nobiel Center. It's his first show."

Larry's brows lifted. "Impressive. He has a sponsor?"

"Stephen Stevens from New York."

"Ah, yes. I believe I've heard of the name. Quite a prestigious business."

"I'm scared. What if he refuses to talk with me? What if he doesn't want to hear my apology?"

The strong face of her new friend grew serious. "We will pray for good results."

Good results were what she wanted. Prayer was definitely what she needed. Caro stared down at her clenched fingers.

"I have an interest in art. Would it help if I went with you, Caro?"

Yes? Or no? "I'd better do this by myself. But it wouldn't hurt for me to see a friendly face there if you decided to go."

"You've got it."

~*~

The private prayer time had helped. Andy's spirits had bounced back, and now he felt ready to enjoy the evening. In spite of Donald's offer to swing by in his fast car and pick him up, Andy had refused. He wanted to be alone.

And he wanted to pick up some gifts. Gifts for his friends and a special gift for Caroline.

Lauren had given him the names of several excellent shops.

Andy's gaze flipped from building to building through the taxi window. The gray, swollen clouds had finally released the rain, and it shimmered in the approaching evening. The taxi driver whipped around a corner, and Andy jumped at the sight of a girl on the arm of a white haired man, with a goatee and mustache, climbing the steps of one of the best hotels in Paris.

His heart pounded. Stretching out an arm, he almost tapped the driver on the shoulder to stop, and then they were past. He swiveled to stare back at the girl and shook his head.

No. It couldn't have been Caroline. Toby would have let him know. He would have known in his heart if she were in Paris.

He settled back in his seat and forced himself to think of the night ahead.

Chapter Twenty-four

Two hours later, the rain-splattered taxi that sped through Paris shone in the streetlights like glazed yellow paint. Caro sat in the back, her stomach quivering, her hands shaking.

You're going to have to stop this. He'll be glad to see you. Toby said so. Trust, trust, trust your instincts. Dear Lord, how do I get in these messes? Help me be strong and steady and let Andy know I really am sorry. Regardless of what happens between us.

The driver swerved to the curb, and Caro stepped out of the car, flipping a bill across the front seat. She threw a word of thanks over her shoulder, but her gaze fixed on the impressive stone building. Lights blazed, classy-looking people exited limousines and expensive cars and hurried to get out of the rain.

Caro swallowed the monstrous lump in her throat and looked down at the gown she wore. Toni had picked it out, had insisted it was perfect for tonight, and Caro was sure she looked as good as any of these other dressed up people.

If only she could convince the country-person inside her of that.

Taking a deep breath, Caro let it out slowly, then climbed the steps, walked inside and felt dwarfed by the high-ceilinged room. The quiet muted music and low hum of voices sent a deluge of panic through her body.

I can't do this. Caro slipped behind a group of people and wished she'd agreed to have Larry accompany her. Too late now. On tiptoe she searched the room for Andy. Where was he? The woman with red hair gave her pause. No, too old for Lauren.

Her gaze flicked over groups and couples, then landed on a group not ten feet from her. She'd never met Stephen Stephens, but the sight of Lauren Stephens, clinging to the arm of the blond guy beside her trim figure, sent her heart into a nosedive. They looked like the perfect couple.

Was that Andy? It had to be.

Broad smiles all around. The guy received several hearty back slaps and a few handshakes. Heads nodded. Laughter floated through the air.

The blond guy turned to speak to someone, and Caro caught his profile. It was Andy. Caro clutched at the tall Corinthian post she leaned against. It was Andy, but a different Andy.

It wasn't the Andy she knew in old comfortable clothes, his hands stained with the oils he loved. It wasn't Andy dressed in his best suit. It wasn't the Andy she'd known all her life, who she'd despised as passive and unemotional and uninteresting.

This Andy looked suave in his expensive-looking tux cut to fit shoulders that suddenly looked wide and strong. Pant creases so sharp they looked razor-like. Polished shoes that reflected vague images.

A man who'd come into his own right in the world he'd been meant to live in. Confident.

Strong. Knowledgeable. Comfortable.

A man, she realized, who was more precious than anything in the world to her. At home, Toby and Toni had convinced her Andy wanted her here. That it was her duty to share the evening with him. But now?

How on earth could little old her approach that group? Would Andy snub her? Would Lauren laugh at her?

Caro eyed the girl. Her gown looked as if it'd been spun from pure gold. Beautiful with all that red hair flung over those bare shoulders. Radiant and happy.

And why wouldn't Andy be fascinated? After all, Lauren was the daughter of his sponsor. Lauren was a sweet, gorgeous girl. Not a country gal who didn't have the sense God gave a goose. She was someone who valued a splendid, talented man.

Andy's head bent, and Lauren stretched up to whisper something in his ear. His head went back, his mouth widened, and though Caro couldn't hear it, she could almost see the laughter pouring from him.

Fingers fumbling for her cell phone, she punched in the long distance number. When Toby's dear voice spoke in her ear, she gasped out, "This was such a mistake. I'm coming home." Before he could dig into her motives, she slammed her finger on the off button and shoved her cell deep into the dainty bag dangling from her arm.

Her gaze flipped to the group mid-way across the room. Caro watched Andy hold out his arm, her tears building, stair-stepping their way up her throat. Lauren tossed a glance at her father, then walked away with Andy Carrington.

And Caro—the real true coward—fled the building.

~*~

Donald was waiting when Andy entered the building and steered him toward some of the mingling guests. When he obviously figured he had Andy securely taken care of, he ambled away. But minutes later, Andy was already bored of the conversation, and excused himself. He avoided Stephens for the moment, not that he particularly wanted to, but because of the attractive red head who was determined to win him over.

Moving toward several tall plants, Andy edged behind them to take a breather before re-entering the gathering.

"You hold off...few months...I can get it for you...much cheaper, of course."

Bending just a bit, Andy strained to hear what was being said. Who was it? Not...Couldn't be.

The men moved away, but in the opposite direction, and unless Andy wanted to make a scene, he'd have to let them go.

It didn't stop him from wondering what the man behind the plants had meant. Wait a few months...for what?

~*~

Andy stared down at the girl at his side. He was happy to see her, but on his guard, too. She could be such a sweet person, but she didn't hesitate to let him know anytime he wanted to be more than friends, she would be willing. He knew Stephens would be anything but disappointed if he showed interest in his daughter.

But he couldn't.

As much as he wanted to please the man, Andy wouldn't play around with Lauren's affections. He knew to whom his heart belonged.

Caroline's color-shifting eyes, her face with the dozen soft, barely seen freckles sprinkled like tan star dust across her nose, never left his thoughts. Her vision refused to leave when he gazed at Lauren, when he discussed art with wealthy prospective buyers of his work, nor when he went to sleep at night and woke the next morning.

His heart refused to forget. His prayers were a constant plea God would soon answer his desire.

Caroline, Caroline, where are you? I need you here. I'm only half a person without you.

He and Lauren rejoined Stephens, and his sponsor guided him across the room to meet yet again another prospect. They talked for fifteen minutes, then Andy's cell phone rang, and he excused himself.

"Did she get there?"

"Who?"

Toby's voice barely held back the excitement. "Caro. She flew out late last night and arrived in Paris today. Haven't you seen her?"

For a moment, Andy could say nothing as his mind froze in confusion.

"Caroline's here? In Paris?" Andy almost

dropped his phone. He swiveled to stare around the room, hoping he'd catch a glimpse of his beloved vision.

"What time is it there?"

Andy glanced down at his watch. "It's nine-thirty. Another half hour and the show will be over."

"Are you saying she's not there?"

"I haven't seen her. Where's she staying?"

When Toby hung up after exacting promises to call him as soon as Andy had located her, Andy called information to get the number of her hotel.

"I believe she took a cab to the Art De Nobiel Center, sir." The calm unenthusiastic voice of the hotel desk clerk offered the tidbit.

Andy hung up and clenched his fingers. Where was she? Had something happened to her?

Punching in Toby's number again, he paced and worried, ignoring the gawking people around him. Busy. He wanted to toss the irritating thing in the trash. Donald slipped up beside him. "What's the matter with you?"

He looked at his agent, opened his mouth to explain, and then snapped it closed. Donald would not understand. "Nothing."

His cell rang, and Andy swerved away. "Hello."

Toby's agitated voice came through the phone. "Andy. Caro just called. She said she's coming home."

"What on earth for?"

"I don't know. She was crying so hard I could hardly hear what she said."

"What was Caroline going to wear tonight?"

"Uh, I don't know. Wait. Toni said something about a blue dress that would make the word 'wow' have a new meaning. That was it. Blue. Why?"

"Never mind. Now tell me, what would be her favorite places to visit here?"

"How am I supposed to know that? Wait. She always talks about the Eiffel Tower at night, and how much she'd love to see it."

"Okay. I'll get back to you. Don't worry. I'll find her."

Stephens was staring at him, displeasure riding his features. Andy strode toward him.

"Is something wrong, my boy? I wanted this evening to be perfect for you."

He wanted to shout nothing would be perfect until Caroline stood by his side, but he didn't. Instead he sent him the best reassuring smile he could paste on his lips. "An emergency's come up. I'm going to have to skip out of our late supper."

His agent blustered a protest. "Andy, I've bent over backwards, from stealing to bribing, to get you here. You want to leave now?"

"I don't want to. I *have* to leave. It's not going to ruin anything to miss our personal dinner." Andy wasn't going to budge. His agent would just have to deal with it.

The lines that appeared between his sponsor's brow told Andy he wasn't pleased. "Is this necessary?"

"Yes, it is. If I can get back in time, I'll meet you at the restaurant." He thrust out a hand. "Thank you, Stephens. It's been a memorable evening. I couldn't have done it without you."

And then he was off. At the door he stopped in front of the doorman and pulled out a picture. "Have you seen her tonight?"

The man started to shake his head. Andy stepped closer. "Look harder, man. Have you seen her?"

The doorman's gaze flicked to the picture. "Oui. She is the girl in the blue dress who cried."

"What are you saying?" Andy grabbed his arm. "Tell me, quick."

"She came alone. Very pretty, and I wondered at her having no escort."

"What did she do?"

"She was here maybe a half-hour, then, in a great rush, leaves." The man spread his hands, and his voice rose and became dramatic in the telling. "Runs out, and I believe the lady was crying. Her cheeks were wet and her eyes...they were anguished eyes."

It was time to leave, and Andy tossed him a twenty.

"There was a gentleman."

The words slapped him in the back. Andy whipped around. "What?"

"The lady ran into a white-haired gentleman outside. He took her arm and led her away."

"Are you sure this is the lady you saw?" Andy tapped the picture in his hand.

"Oui, monsieur. I am sure."

Andy ran outside, and flagged a cab.

"Where you headed, man?"

"Go to the Crowne Plaza Paris Champs Elysées."

"Right."

It took ten minutes but seemed more like an

eternity before the taxi screeched to a halt in front of the hotel. Andy swung open the door. "Wait."

Striding into the building, Andy headed toward the reception desk. "Excuse me, I'm looking for Caroline Gibson. I believe she has a room here. Has she returned?"

The man tapped on the keyboard in front of him. "Let me check her room, sir."

His impatient fingers drummed on the countertop, mentally counting the rings. At last the clerk hung up the receiver. "She's not answering, sir. She must still be out."

"Please try again," Andy urged.

With a longsuffering sigh, the clerk obeyed. When he hung up again, he insisted. "I'm sorry. Would you like to leave a note?"

"Not now. I'll be back."

The waiting taxi still idled by the curb. Where to go? *Lord, where should I look for her?* She would...what? Think, Andy, think. He knew Caroline. What would she do if she were upset?

Walk. She would try to walk it out of her system. "Let's head to the Seine River."

Dear Lord, help me find her, and I'll never let her go again.

The wipers swished back and forth on the windshield as the driver sped through the streets, the drizzle picking up on the lights and brightening the scenes. Andy fastened his gaze on the passing scenery, afraid he'd miss her but felt no lightening of his spirits.

Had Caroline seen him beside Lauren and chickened out?

And who on earth was the white-haired gentleman?

Chapter Twenty-five

Caro slammed into a solid body and heard the involuntary grunt that escaped from lips surrounded by a well-trimmed mustache. Hands gripped her forearms, and a warm voice filled her ears, but she could hear little but the buzz of her own tortured thoughts.

"What is the matter, my young friend?"

She shook her head, and the friendly face of Larry Merle blurred.

"Come, my dear." He turned and flagged a car.

Her elderly friend instructed his driver but Caro paid no attention. When he sat back, she looked out the side window, dejection and embarrassment struggling for supremacy in her feelings. She let her head drop into her hands and groaned. "Silly, silly. How could I be so ridiculous?"

Larry pulled her hands from her face. "Would you like to tell me what happened? Did you talk with your Andy, and he refused to listen?"

"He didn't have a chance."

"Because—?"

"I chickened out. When I saw him there, it was like seeing a different person. Someone I didn't know. He was at home, laughing, and happier than I've seen him in a long time. Beautiful people around him, vying for his attention."

The old minister sat with bowed head for so long Caro finally ventured a glance at him.

At last he spoke. "Forgive me, but are you not taking the reins of your life into your hands again? Did we not pray God would go before you to smooth the way for your apology to your friend? How do you know but what this act from you would have eased a hurt in his heart?"

The man's words, soft and low, nevertheless wedged like a sword of conviction in her heart. She had failed yet another time. Why couldn't she get anything right?

"Would you mind if I got out now?" She drew in a shaky breath. "I'd like to walk and think for awhile."

"Are you sure?" One eyebrow lifted as Larry's gaze rested on the rain outside the vehicle. "You will get wet."

"I'll be fine. I'll walk just a little, then get a taxi back to the hotel."

Larry leaned forward and tapped the driver on the shoulder. "Please stop the car, Pauley."

When the car had pulled over, Caro opened the door. "Thank you, Larry, for your advice and prayers."

The minister nodded. "Be careful, my dear."

The taxi pulled away, and Caro studied the street ahead of her then headed down the lane, his wise advice echoing in her mind, her heart heavy at the memory of Lauren and Andy together at the art center. One thing for sure, she'd gotten no vibes Andy was lonely for her.

Larry was right. She *had* wimped out because of her imagination. Instead of *trusting*

God to smooth the way before her, she had charged *Andy* as guilty in behaving as badly as she usually did. And he hadn't even known she was there. She'd taken the reins of decision from his hands—and God's—and made the decision herself.

God, forgive me. Give me one last chance.

~*~

"Stop right here."

The taxi driver swerved to the bank of the Seine River, stomped on the brakes till they screamed for mercy, and started to speak.

He had no time to listen to unwanted advice. Andy slammed his door open. "Wait."

He stepped out of the car, stood on the sidewalk and watched the adorable figure trudging through the drizzle, half a block away. It had to be her. Silhouetted against the beautiful golden lights of the avenue, she was small, vulnerable and alone. A dejected, rain-soaked, blue gown-clad figure.

The most beloved sight in the world to him.

Andy wanted to run to her.

Instead he walked steadily toward her, his heart beating in tempo with the words exploding inside him. He was twenty-five feet behind her when he began singing, softly at first, then with increasing volume. "You're a woman who is my fantasy and yet you're my reality. You're everything to me. You're a woman to me."

Caroline stopped walking as suddenly as if she'd run into a stone wall. What was she thinking? Did she know it was he, singing to her? Walking to her?

"You're everything I need. You're everything to me."

She whirled, her face a mask of disbelief, and Andy thought his heart would burst.

"You're every woman in the world to me."

"Andy?"

He couldn't hear her whispered word, but he saw it on her lips, and he held out his arms.

Hesitation flickered across her features, then hope. She began the long walk to him, and he watched her come.

He took ten steps, strolling and singing, meeting her halfway, his heart in his untrained voice. He saw her, through the misting rain, pick up her pace until she was running straight for him, crying his name over and over. Beautiful, beautiful music to his ears.

When she reached him, she threw herself at him, and he caught her, gathered her close, his arms closing around her. "You're every woman in the world to me, Caroline." He sang to her.

"I'm sorry. I'm sorry." She murmured the words over and over.

With her face pressed against his chest, his lips brushed her wet hair and murmured the vow to her heart. "I'll never let you go."

~*~

"This was better than any show." The cabbie's broad, round face beamed at the two thoroughly soaked lovers.

When they'd finally come out of their own world, Andy had looked up to see the driver had pulled up beside them and leaned over to watch with intense interest the scenario unfolding.

Andy didn't care. With Caroline's hand in

his, he pressed the bill into the gawking cabbie's hand and motioned him away.

The driver rolled his window all the way down. "Say, if you're going to be here long, give me a call. I'd love to drive you anywhere." The window shot up and with a screech, he took off.

They walked then, arm in arm. The night grew cooler, the street crowd, with their colorful umbrellas and more somber rain gear, grew thinner, and still they talked and walked. When they reached the Eiffel Tower, they began climbing and at the second level, they stood in the misting rain and leaned out over the night-lit city.

At one point, Caroline drew in a breath. "I need to say this, Andy, then I'll never bring it up again." She stayed within his arms, but kept her gaze on the water below them.

"You do know you don't have to." He brushed a rain-darkened strand from her face, tucking it behind a perfect ear.

"Yes, I do have to say this. I can't tell you how I felt when I sent you away. It was bad enough I'd committed such a horrible deed, but to know my thoughtless words had...injured you, was almost more than I could stand for this past long month."

Her voice broke, and Andy started to speak, to reassure her, but she stopped him. "No, I know you want to make it easy for me, that you want me to forget it, but I can't yet. I've got to be woman enough to finish."

She searched his face, and he signaled he understood with his own look.

"I want you to know I was sorry from the moment I left you, but I can never explain *how* sorry. My anger at you and my stubbornness in wanting my own way hindered me from knowing God's perfect will for me and my life. I think God grew impatient with the dream world I lived in and jerked the rose-colored glasses from my eyes. Only then did I realize what I was missing."

He wanted to stop her frantic words, wishing he could ease the hurt in her.

"I really thought maybe I'd gone too far for you to forgive me. And when I saw the way..."

Her throat contracted as she swallowed, and he loved the mesmerizing action.

"...the way Lauren looked at you, I nearly died. I mean she's beautiful and sophisticated and—"

"And have I told you what a cute nose you have? Your lashes are thick and dark, a perfect foil for those dreamy eyes of yours. In fact, you are wonderful tonight. How could I love anyone but you?" Andy brushed a finger over her face, then bent to touch her lips with his own.

When he released her, she teased. "Truly, Andy?"

"I love you, Caroline. And for your information, don't let any of that bother you again. It's forgiven and forgotten. I've never loved another woman and never considered anyone but you. You are the only woman in the world for me."

He pulled her closer beside him. "Now, I want to know. Would you like to come back to Paris for our honeymoon?"

~*~

"Can you do it?"

Detective Eddie dragged out his sigh as if his patience had reached a limit, but Caro new better. The man never, ever lost his cool with his friends. She reckoned she fit that description.

"I suppose, for you, I can look into it. Tell me again why this is so important."

"It might lead me to the person who stole Andy's paintings." Wouldn't that be the perfect wedding present for him? She could see his face...

"And I have to rule out everyone. You know how that goes, Eddie."

"Okay, I'll squeeze the job in for you seeing as how it's more important than the other twenty-five cases I have stacked on my desk."

Caro squealed. "Oooo. I love you, Eddie. You'll get a front row seat at our wedding!"

"I'd just better." His good-natured chuckle echoed in her ears as she hung up.

~*~

Andy picked up his magnifying glass again and re-studied the pictures he'd had printed off his phone. It had to be. That tall form, the heavy build. But why?

Tucking the glass safely in a drawer, he stacked the three pictures in order, all the while pondering.

If it was who he suspected—and he put that together with the voice in Paris promising results in weeks, then it didn't bode well for the person. He was disappointed and sad, but what else could he do? If he was wrong, would it be an irreversible situation, neither could handle?

Probably.

But he had to know for sure.

He picked up his phone and punched in a number.

“Detective Eddie?”

Chapter Twenty-six

"How's my girl this morning?" Andy's voice glowed with happiness.

Caroline sat down at Undiscovered Treasure's counter and clutched the receiver closer to her ear. She waved at Toby to go away.

"Aren't you painting?"

"Yes, but I wondered if you could come on out around eleven? I have a surprise for you."

"I can't wait. Tell me now." Curiosity jumped inside her like a Mexican jumping bean.

Andy's laugh rang through the receiver, and Caroline adored the sound.

"No. You, my sweet, soon-to-be wife will just have to rein in that insatiable curiosity of yours and wait."

She replaced the phone and strolled over to the ballerina music box.

Toby stuck his head out of his office. "Andy?"

"He asked me to stop by at eleven."

"Go." Toby sighed. "I might as well agree. I'll not get any more work out of you today now that you've talked to him."

"It's about time you're doing some work around here."

She arrived fifteen minutes early. Stephanie opened the door to her knock. "Go on into his studio. He's waiting for you."

Caroline stepped into the room, and her gaze flew straight to the man she loved. He looked far from the elegant man he'd been at Paris. Now, in his slouchy sweatshirt and ragged jeans, he looked the part of a pauper artist, making his way in the world.

Warmth spread through her. She loved both Andy's. How could she not?

"Hey, you're early. Good. Come on in."

"What's the surprise?"

"First things first. Come with me. We're going to get to the bottom of my..." He gave her a knowing look as he whispered the rest. Taking her hand, he laced his fingers through hers and led her to his sitting room.

Inside, Stephanie Leason hovered over a table, pouring coffee into four cups. Donald Snelling stood by a window, shifting from foot to foot as if the waiting was almost more than he could stand. He turned when they entered.

"Andy, I hope you've got a good reason to call me here in the middle of the week.

"Oh, I do, Donald. I do. But first, I'd like you to meet my fiancée, Caroline Gibson. Caroline, my agent, Donald Snelling." Andy motioned for Caroline to take a seat. "It's about something I'm sure you both will be happy to learn."

Stephanie's brows drew together in a frown, but she didn't speak.

"And since both of you work with Andy, he wanted you two to be the first to know." Caroline tossed in the information, forcing her voice to stay calm. After all, this was Andy's story, his victory over greedy thieves.

"Caroline and I found out who stole my

paintings."

"What?" Andy's agent's face had turned an ugly shade of red. Was he angry over the news or concerned?

"The thing is," Andy swiveled to face Stephanie who sat on the edge of her seat. "I was sure God had sent me a double blessing when I hired you. You're smart and efficient and kept me organized."

The pause was pregnant with–was it suspense or fear?

"You think too much so, Andy?" Caro couldn't keep quiet. Her spirits were bouncing with happiness in helping Andy do this.

"I do, dear Caroline."

Andy was the sweetest thing in the world. Why hadn't she ever seen it before?

"That's why, when Caroline and I saw you holding the huge, flat package and talking with a couple of men, I wondered what was going on. You remember, don't you?"

"But you weren't even that concerned, if I remember correctly, my love." Caro almost chuckled. They were laying it on pretty thick. When would the other two realize they were laughing at—never mind. Andy was talking again.

"True. But it did make me think." He eyed his assistant. "You see. I'm smart too, Stephanie—or at least Caroline insists I am, and I'm inclined to take her word for it—" he grinned. "It didn't take me long to check my records. I hadn't asked you to send or deliver any of my paintings that date or anytime close to that date. I wasn't expecting to send any out for two weeks later. And why would you be shipping paintings?"

"I can explain."

"I hope you can, because I—we—really want to hear it."

"I forgot to mail the one you wanted to send to Regency's." Stephanie lowered her gaze. "I was afraid to tell you. Afraid you'd be angry."

"Stephanie, do you really expect me to believe that? You know I'm not a person easily riled, and I certainly understand forgetfulness. At times."

"The problem with your explanation is..." Caroline leaned forward. "...we checked with Regency's, and they received the painting exactly when they were supposed to. That means, you're lying to us. There has to be another explanation."

Stephanie said nothing, her mouth set in a mulish expression.

Andy was talking again, and Caro focused on her man.

"After that, we checked with Detective Eddie. Had him do some, uh, background search on you. Can you guess what we found out? We were shocked, to say the least."

"Remember when we first met? At the time I thought it odd you'd stop at the house and ask if I needed an assistant. Quite out of the blue. How often does that happen?"

The assistant opened and shut her mouth.

"But it wasn't just the package. You see I overheard a conversation you had, and since I've been very paranoid, you might call it, since the thefts began, I had a company keep track of all calls coming and going from my work phone. Now, that was odd, putting it together with the conversation, to find out you'd been talking—behind my back, mind you, to—"

"That's illegal."

"I didn't ask permission, no, but I don't need the telephone information anyway, so we won't be using it. Don't worry about that." Andy stood and walked to the window. "You see, I know who tried to kill me with one of your Uncle Bennett's cars. Yes, he and his driver have alibis, so it wasn't them. Who else could it have been? You? Don't shake your head. With your uncle's permission, Detective Eddie and his officers dusted for fingerprints. Whose do you think was in the car, Stephanie?"

"I have no idea."

"I think you do."

"And to think my suspicion of you after seeing you with the flat package is what sent me to Detective Eddie. You see, I'm not quite as easy-going as my future husband is. Still, he's a wonderful person." Caro turned to Andy and gave him an admiring look before asking him, "Officer Eddie's the one good officer in the force, don't you think?"

"He's the best."

"After I convinced Eddie I was serious, and the situation was serious, he agreed to look into your past."

"Why did you do it?" Andy's brow puckered. "I trusted you. In fact, I've never done you any harm."

"You haven't? Think again. You may not remember me, but I remember you. Very well." Stephanie's lips curled, the fire in her body radiating so intensely it could have burned a hole in the blouse she wore if it'd touched it. "No one had a chance in our college art class. *You* were the *chosen* one, the one our instructor held up for our admiration of your talents. You were the one who won every award the only year I could afford to go. You were the one who received the job offers before you graduated. No one, and I mean no one, had a chance with you there."

"Was he supposed to do less than his best because of others?" Where was this crazy girl coming off?

"Do you know what Instructor McCoy called my work—the best I'd ever done? All my friends said so. Mediocre. Mediocre, that's what he said with that hateful smirk he reserved for those he really disliked in his class."

For a moment, Caroline's heart beat with compassion. How often had she felt the same discouragement when she knew she wasn't doing anything outstanding? But then she'd never plotted and planned to profit from someone else's hard work either.

That was the difference.

"But it was so long ago. Why would you take your disappointment out on Andy after all these years?"

"Do you think I've forgotten? That I would forget? I've followed him and waited for the right timing to destroy him. Why do think I did such an extreme makeover? Changed my hair color, lost some weight, and bought the clothes I needed. Did the trick, don't you think?" His soon-to-be-fired assistant glared at Caro.

"Tricked him, I'd say. He never recognized me, which suited me just fine. If he wanted to keep me from getting the applause I deserved for *my* work, then he owed me."

Really? The gall of the crooked.

"But he didn't owe you."

"Oh, yes, he did. I already explained to you. If he'd only had sympathy for everyone but himself, he'd have seen how the rest of us were being ignored. I wouldn't be surprised if his family bribed old McCoy to get him the attention."

Andy tried to object, but there was no stopping the woman.

"I've been watching him for years, keeping track because I meant to have some of his money. After I got enough—can a girl ever have too much?—then I planned to see what destruction I could make of his fame." She stretched and stood. "I'm outta here."

"I don't think so." Andy's voice boded no good for the female thief.

"You can't prove anything. I certainly won't tell you where the paintings are, and without them your detective can't prove a thing."

"Are you sure? Your Great Uncle Bennett squealed like a pig. He gave you up."

Andy's glance at her quickened Caro's heartbeat, but she swiveled her gaze back to the malevolent woman in front of her. "Your uncle was never too keen on your idea, and the more he understood your intention, the less he liked it. He's made his amends to Andy. Now it's your turn."

Her lips firmed, and she tossed her head as

if to say, “Never!” But as Detective Eddie and another policeman entered the room, her glance shot to the window. Too late. The detectives slipped handcuffs on her wrists before she could make a move.

The three were almost out the door when she threw back her final comment, never looking back. “Don't think I'll forget. There'll be another time.”

“How does she think she's going to do such a crazy thing?” Donald Snelling shifted in his seat and crossed his legs. “Glad you're rid of her. I never said anything, but couldn't stand her. We'll start with a clear slate, my boy.”

“I'm not your boy, Donald. Get that straight once and for all.” Andy leaned forward. “Now, Donald, I want you to explain to us what your actions were in Stephanie's scheme.”

If her chin had actually hit the floor this time, Caroline wouldn’t have been any more surprised. She stared at Andy, then at Donald. The man certainly looked guilty. His face flushed, but he didn’t lose his composure.

“Why would you think I'd want to have anything to do with her? I already told you I couldn't stand her.”

“Something you said at my show in Paris.”

The quizzical look that crossed Don’s face told Caro he had no idea what he’d let slip.

“Hold off for a few months? You were talking, I believe, to some clients who thought they could buy one of my paintings from you, at a far cheaper price. Am I right so far?”

Donald sagged into the nearest chair.

“When I thought about it, everything made sense that you had a hand in helping her.”

Andy's eyes were truly puzzled. "I can't figure out why. You had already gotten me the Regency's contract and the potential promise of meeting with Stephens. Why, Donald, why? When things were going so well?"

"That's nonsense. Ridiculous. I would never—"

"Unlike Stephanie's situation, I know I won't ever be able to pinpoint your participation. But I know it, and you do. I kept thinking about the man with Stephanie that day on the street. Caroline took pictures, and when she showed them to me, I thought to myself, he looked an awfully lot like you. Enlarged prints proved it."

Andy sat back now and tapped his fingers together. Caroline couldn't take her eyes off him. He was showing his confident, man-of-the-world side, and she loved it. The passion she felt for her man grew.

"Here's what I think went through your head. You're such a successful person you were determined I wouldn't languish in the country, so you worked hard and helped me get these contracts. But when you saw how much I would be making, what attention I was getting, you thought, 'why shouldn't I have more? I've done all the hard work,' forgetting I'm the one who did the painting and gave you the considerable percentage you demanded. That's when Stephanie approached you—no, wait, did you do your own checking up on her? Found out she was an old college colleague of mine with a grudge, and what? Did you see her take one of the paintings? I'm pretty sure blackmail wouldn't be above you. Great opportunity to cash in on some easy cash. All you had to do was hold on to them until I became known, and with your contacts, I'm sure you knew plenty of people who'd pay prime price underground. Am I close?"

"You don't have to say anything. We can see Andy's right." Caroline tossed in for good measure.

Donald's gaze flicked to Caroline, dismissed her as the lesser of two evils and moved back to Andy.

"You've got it wrong. You wouldn't be where you are today if it wasn't for me."

"Maybe I wouldn't, but you're the one wrong this time. I don't need someone I can't trust, and I no longer trust you." Andy stood. "You'll find an envelope addressed to you on the end table in the hallway. It's what I owe you paid in full. Take it and leave. I no longer need or want your services."

"You can't fire me—"

"I can, and I just did. Good-by, Donald, before I decide to have Detective Eddie investigate you a little more fully."

Donald swayed, his blood-shot eyes suddenly strained, his hands clenching and unclenching. "You'll be sorry about this. You can't make it on your own."

"We'll see." The lines crinkling at the corners of Andy's eyes caused Caro's mouth to go dry.

Chapter Twenty-seven

Caro rested her head on Andy's shoulder. "You were wonderful."

"Only because of your help."

"Maybe." She lifted her head and grinned up at him. "Now can I have my surprise?"

"Don't you want to wait until tomorrow?"

Scowling wouldn't help, but she tried it anyway, then burst out laughing when he pretended to whistle silently and ignore her.

He led her over to one of his pictures. "We, my dear sweetheart, are having an art lesson today. I want you to see and feel what I do when I create these paintings."

"Andy, I'm not smart about art. I just don't get it."

"You will."

His confident tone sent her own confidence level to the top.

"Okay. Let's study this one. What do you see?"

"A wagon train circled by Indians."

"Who's winning?"

"Looks like the Native Americans are."

"Look closer." At her vague glance, he pointed. "Over here in the corner."

Caro leaned into the picture. "Why, it looks like a bunch of soldiers."

Satisfaction edged Andy's voice. "Right. There is hope in sight for the losing train."

He moved to another one. "Now this one."

"I see a raging fire devouring a forest." Caro followed close behind him. "Firefighters with defeated faces. And..."

Her gaze roved over the picture. "There. Is it the storm clouds approaching? Rain's on its way. You've made them so subtly separate from the heavy smoke."

They went from one to another, and Caroline could see the touch of hope, safety, and rescue Andy had given each one. No more than a hint of it, but it was there. A promise that nothing was ever too bad, but what it could get better.

"They're wonderful, Andy. I can't believe I didn't ever see that."

"Partly my fault. I should have insisted on explaining it to you."

"You don't ever have to worry about me again, Andy."

"I know." His heart was in his eyes when he said, "One more painting you need to see."

"You don't have to show me more. I understand your work now."

No answer, but he slowly made his way around to another easel and tossed back its covering.

Caro walked slowly toward it, her hand outstretched, stunned at the passionate emotion emulating from it. It was a painting of herself, and for a moment, she couldn't turn from it. Not because of the subject—herself—but because of Andy's feelings he'd poured into each stroke.

Then in a rush, she ran to him, tears in her eyes, her mouth wide in a shy smile. "Why,

Andy? Why did you do it?"

"You don't know? Look at me and then say, you don't know. I know the exact spot where my favorite painting will hang in our home."

"You do? You've already decided?"

"Uh, huh. If I waited on you, you'd decide to sell it."

She stroked his cheek, her finger moving to the slight dimple in his chin. "Andy, that is the best gift anyone has ever given me."

He started to answer, but she shook her head. "Not because of the painting itself, but because I can feel your love in it."

Andy drew her close. "Have I told you lately you're the dearest thing in the world to me?"

"Tell me again, Andy."

She'd never get tired of hearing it.

Chapter Twenty-eight

Her wedding party encircled their table. Caro wanted all of them to hear and purposely raised her voice as she leaned across the table to speak to Toni. "Can I borrow a pen and paper?"

She was aware of her friends' gazes on her as she scribbled on the plain paper.

Aware and glad of it. She wanted all of them to see this. To see how much she adored Andy. He was hers, and she was thrilled at that thought.

It took her several minutes to get the words just like she wanted them, but when she finished, she signed it with a flourish and handed it to Andy. "A short note to Linc."

His quick frown had her smiling with happiness. His instant jealousy was endearing.

"Am I allowed to know why my wife is writing to this guy? A good enough guy on his own, but one I'm not too fond of because of his mistaken interest in a certain woman I love."

A giggle escaped her even though she strove for seriousness. She batted her lashes at him. "Silly. I gave you the note. Read it aloud and learn, dear hubby."

For a moment Andy continued to gaze at her, then glanced down and read what his new bride had written. His voice was wonderfully brisk and disbelieving as he whispered.

Dear Linc, I wanted you to know I've decided to sell the ballerina music box after all. It's no longer significant to me, nor does it suit the store's persona. If you're still interested, I'll be glad to ship it to you as soon as possible..."

"And why wouldn't you want this music box anymore?"

"If you knew me so well, you'd know why." She couldn't resist teasing him and nudged him with her shoulder. "It's no longer a symbol of my life."

"Why is that?"

Caro wrinkled her nose at the dearest man in the world to her. "I'm thinking of getting a big smiley face and pasting it up in the window of Undiscovered Treasures as a symbol of my heart's continual state."

"Really, Caroline?" Andy leaned close to her.

"Really. And I'm Caro. It's time for you to remember." Caro edged toward him and allowed her lips to be captured, loving the taste of him and inhaling the scent of his rich cologne.

He was whispering in her ear. "Never, my love. From now on, you're Caroline to the world. As you've always been to me."

The laughter and the banging on the tables was only faint background music to the words singing in her heart. Andy's words. His declaration of love for her.

You're every woman in the world to me.

Ah, yes. She wasn't spinning any more. She'd found her purpose...and Andy.

Carole Brown

Undiscovered Treasures

Toby's Troubles

An Appleton, WV Romantic Mystery

Chapter One

Toby Gibson didn't believe in ghosts.

Or at least he hadn't until recently. But unusual sounds, open windows and unlocked doors made for a pretty convincing case that something very strange was going on. Especially when nothing seemed to be disturbed or stolen.

Slowly, he opened his eyes—but just a crack—and shifted his gaze from one side to the other as far as he could see.

Which wasn't far, seeing as it was pitch black in his bedroom. Just the way he liked it. But if he was going to snag the current ghost in his home, he was going to have to forget about getting spooked if he did happen to see it.

He chuckled, sat up, and reached for the flashlight he'd placed on his night stand just in case the Undiscovered Treasures' ghost decided to show up again. Flashing it around the room, he saw nothing unusual. Hmmm. Did that mean it had moved on to a more exciting home?

Not if the faint, faint sounds coming from the first floor were any indication.

Toby swung his legs to the floor and stood, edging as quietly as he could in his bare feet to the door. He twisted the knob and peered through the crack, but only a dim nightlight illumined the short hallway.

Twice before he'd tried to catch Undiscovered

Treasurer's ghost, but had failed. Maybe the third time would be the charm he needed. Stepping as softly as he could, he headed to the stairs and took one step at a time, making sure to avoid the second from the bottom that squeaked as noisily as a mouse would when caught in a trap by the tail.

At the bottom, Toby drew in a deep breath. The sounds were coming from a side room where he always placed the newest items he'd found and bought so they could be inventoried and priced before placed in the main section of the store.

An unusually loud noise had him mentally perking his ears. What on earth was the thing doing? He'd soon find out.

Tiptoeing, unlit flashlight still in hand, Toby moved toward the room. The door was cracked a hair, and he paused, listening.

A slight scooting sound as if it was pushing something...or was it a drawer opening? Then a faint ruffling sound. Was it sifting through something and allowing it to fall gently back into the container? Rummaging through cloth?

Toby gave the door an easy shove. Across the room, a light shone on an antique cabinet that needed a touch of repair before he and Caroline could sell it. Doors were opening and shutting.

So dark was the windowless room, Toby could see nothing but that bit of light shining here and there on the cabinet. He had no idea what the ghost looked like or whether it was a bad ghost or good one.

A chuckle spilled from his throat at the thought, and the ghost whirled, shining the light directly into his eyes, blinding him.

He heard the ghost coming, felt its nearness, and without pausing to think, Toby lifted and struck out at the thing with his flashlight as it passed him.

A raspy grunt.

The sound of staggering feet.

A growl.

And the thing ran down the hall, ducked into the main selling room, and by the sound of it, slammed open the front door, and without bothering to slam it shut, left without a word.

That was pretty callous out of the—well, he was going to say ghost, but now, having met him in a manner of sorts, he'd have to say—person. The least the fellow could have done was say 'hi,' or 'thanks for letting me search your business.'

Or explain what he was doing.

Or looking for.

Other Books by Carole Brown

Women's Fiction:
The Redemption of Caralynne Haymen

Misc
West Virginia Scrapbook

Denton and Alex Davies Mysteries:
Hog Insane
Bat Crazy

Spies of World War II
With Music In Their Hearts

The Appleton Mysteries
Sabotaged Christmas
Knight in Shining Apron

Award winning author Carole Brown loves to weave suspense and tough topics into her books, along with a touch of romance and whimsy.

She is always on the lookout for outstanding titles and catchy ideas.

Carole and Dan, her pastor husband, reside in SE Ohio and have ministered and counseled across the country. Together, they enjoy their grandsons, traveling, gardening, good food, the simple life, and did she mention their grandsons?

Carole loves to connect with her readers. You can find her at her blog:

Sunnebnkwrtr.blogspot.com/

And facebook:

www.facebook.com/CaroleBrown.author

If you enjoyed reading this book, please let others know...and bless Carole Brown with an honest review.

www.ingramcontent.com/pod-product-compliance
Lightning Source LLC
Chambersburg PA
CBHW031703170626
46808CB00005B/1591

* 9 7 8 1 9 4 1 6 2 2 3 8 4 *